Rapture River

A NOVEL

Robert Edward Smith

outskirts
press

Rapture River
All Rights Reserved.
Copyright © 2025 Robert Edward Smith
v2.0

This is a work of fiction. Names, characters, businesses, places, events, locales, and incidents are either the products of the author's imagination or used in a fictitious manner. Any resemblance to actual persons, living or dead, or actual events is purely coincidental.

The opinions expressed in this manuscript are solely the opinions of the author and do not represent the opinions or thoughts of the publisher. The author has represented and warranted full ownership and/or legal right to publish all the materials in this book.

This book may not be reproduced, transmitted, or stored in whole or in part by any means, including graphic, electronic, or mechanical without the express written consent of the publisher except in the case of brief quotations embodied in critical articles and reviews.

Outskirts Press, Inc.
http://www.outskirtspress.com

ISBN: 978-1-9772-7512-7

Cover Photo © 2025 www.gettyimages.com. All rights reserved - used with permission.

Outskirts Press and the "OP" logo are trademarks belonging to Outskirts Press, Inc.

PRINTED IN THE UNITED STATES OF AMERICA

Dedication

For Alice Carol

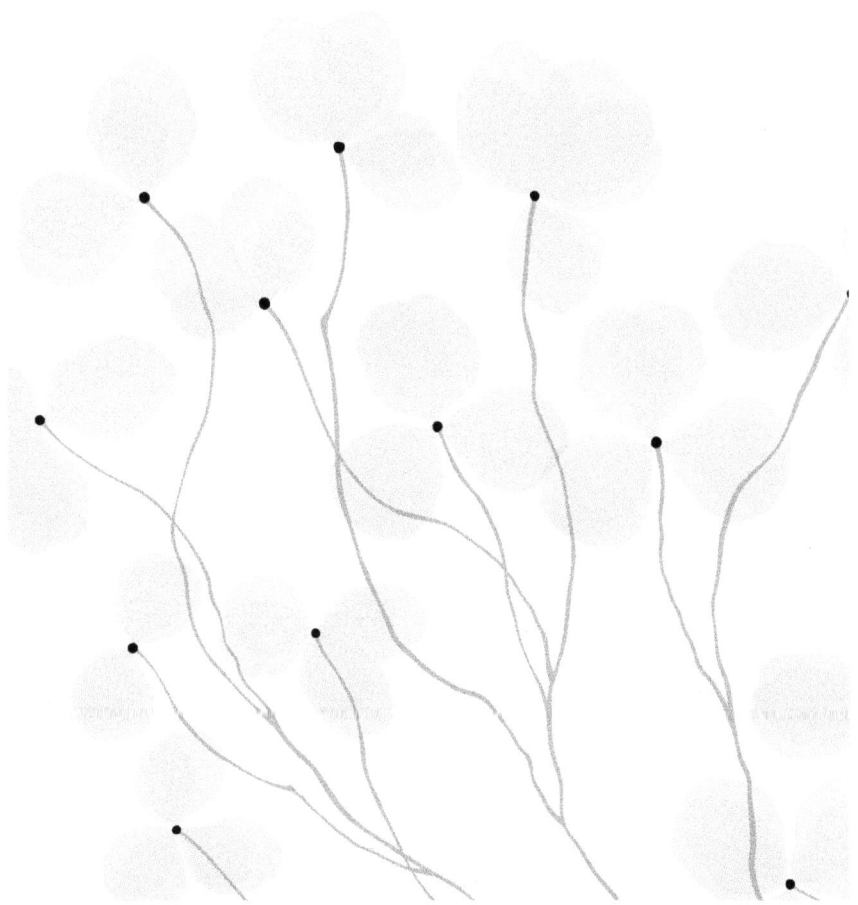

Epigraph

"The leap between the sacred and profane is as thin as fishing line; and is part of the mystery on this river of life…"[1] —Joy Harjo, an enrolled member of the Muscogee Tribe, from *The Woman Who Fell from the Sky: Poems.*

---

1 Harjo, Joy, *The Woman Who Fell from The Sky: Poems* (Copyright 1994 by Joy Harjo, First published as a Norton paperback 1996) p. 75, e-book, "Fishing." Used by permission.

Author's Note to the Reader

Rapture River is a work of fiction. However, the Black River is not a fantasy. It exists and plays a dynamic presence in the novel. I remain steadfast in my viewpoint that it—the Black River—is a she.

She originates in springs near the settlement of Johannesburg in northern Michigan, flows north to join the Cheboygan River, and together they empty into Lake Huron. As the crow flies, she covers a distance of fifty miles; as the river runs, over one hundred miles. She has the reputation as a premier fly-fishing river for brook trout.

The section of the river that streams through the novel is a mere four or five miles.

In that stretch the story gushes out in foamy rapids, deep, bottomless pools, and swirling eddies that force the river and story to flashback upon itself. As variable as Michigan's weather, the river can be as wide as a three-lane highway, or as narrow as one lane and flanked by banks, forcing the current to funnel through. She's blessed with riverbed covered with a ruffled sheet of gravel and sand, so she's easy to wade—the surest way to her heartbeat. One side may be eight feet deep, while the middle, knee-deep; the shallows on the opposite side, a few inches with mounds of dry gravel. Adjacent hillsides are scattered with white and red pines. In flatter parts, cedar trees, deeply rooted into the shoreline hillock, lean over the water, adding shade and aroma. In low-lying areas, the river, angry with rain, will overflow into mucky-scented swamps.

And then, when she drains and heals these marshlands, her clearness is flooded with a muddy black, thus her name.

Part 1

Chapter 1

Midstream. Josh stood in his insulated waders, braced against the waist-high current. He lowered his hand into the water to unhook his fly from a weed. The coldness was numbing. He unwound line from his reel to cast.

High above the river, mayflies were swarming, flapping their transparent, cream-colored wings like miniature angels. This mild spring afternoon was perfect for hatching. Josh was fascinated with these scrappy little creatures and their life-death cycle. And he was drawn into the enchantment of the end and beginning of their short lives. They had survived another cruel Michigan winter beneath ice floes as squirmy little water worms. Under water for a year, they wriggle out from gravel on the bottom and muck along the shorelines, float to the surface, cast off their skins, and sprout wings, all in a matter of minutes—the miracle of birth, he'd say. Then they'd fly off to bank-side grass and leaves and mature into breeding adults in a few days, maybe a week. And he hit it just right as they were spinning over the river, mating, and dipping down onto the water to lay their eggs and die.

Josh cast above a deep pool against an overhanging bank. His Royal Coachman brushed grass and hung on a blade until he teased it onto the current. Floating high on the water, the fly hesitated momentarily, drifted until caught by an eddy, then whirled toward the bank and spun under the drooping grass. He felt it was snagged until it glided out and sailed on.

Joyce was downstream in deep water near the bank, untangling her line from the alders that leaned over the river, all of her 100 pounds holding steady against the current, nearly overflowing the top of her chest-high waders. She looked up and waved.

Josh smiled, nodded, and hoped she'd keep her balance, as daring as she was. In that instant, a brook trout struck, sucked in his Royal Coachman, splashed water against the bank, and rushed upstream toward a logjam. He tightened his fists around the graphite rod, one hand on the butt and the other below the first ferrule, and held it high. *My God, he is big!*

Upriver the rapids roiled into a mist and resounded against the hills and white pines. He drew in line and tugged at the trout's run upstream to avoid the entangling logjams. The fish responded by heading downriver. Josh splashed through sandy shallows and chased the trout as line spun off his reel.

Joyce had waded to a sandbar that jutted out from the deep pool where Josh was struggling to guide the trout. She had laid her fly rod on the bank and held her net above water.

"Don't try to net him," Josh shouted over the rapids, but his words were muffled.

As the fish swayed toward her, she raised the net high and thrust it down, hitting the olive-brown back, the brook trout diving to the bottom with its last outpouring of rage, breaking the 4X tippet.

Josh froze midstream, his rod straight, the limp line waving on the current.

Joyce shrugged, took her broad-brimmed black hat off, laid it against her chest, and bowed.

He was tempted to clap but didn't. This was no place for applauding her clumsiness. She hid behind that bold front to conceal her guilt. Make light of it. She'd never say "I'm sorry." Josh trudged over to the bank and sat down on a whitewashed log that lay in the shallows.

Joyce slowly trod upstream, white foam swirling around her waders. Her thick braid of black hair, now damp, lay over her shoulder, glistening in the late afternoon sun, and her reddish-brown complexion glowed through the prism of the river's mist. When she reached the log, she straddled it in the shallow water and sat down with her back to him, both legs spread into the trickling flow, a wide berth between them.

Josh brushed his hand along the smooth, weathered surface of the log, restraining his anger. Maybe he had expected too much. They had fished together many times, but today was their first outing this year. She had recently turned thirty and was anxious about the approaching decade; he had recently celebrated roaming through five years of that decade—an enjoyable journey, he had assured her. All her Native American sisters were married with children. And she had her dreams of a family.

Gathering above was a flock of swallows chirping *pret pret*, feasting on the swarming mayflies. The couple both looked up, hypnotized by the aerial acrobatics—twisting, dipping, ascending, and descending like little roller coasters.

Staring at the swallows, Josh finally said, "That was the biggest brook trout I ever had on."

She turned toward him, swung her leg over the log, knelt down in the shallows, folded her hands as if in prayer, and said, "Bless me, Father, for I have sinned."

"Yes, and very grievously."

She slapped her hat against the log. "And just what did you mean by that, Father Joshua? When you were a priest, did you ever refuse absolution?"

"That's too long ago to remember."

"Only two years."

She struggled to pull her knees out of the sucking wet sand, the river bottom bubbling up around her, fizzing out its mucky scent. She stood, balanced herself on the log, and stepped toward him. She slipped and he caught her. Settling down by his side, she pressed her thigh against his. With her hand on his knee, she laughed. "Who did you think I was? The Blessed Virgin?"

"I knew you weren't the first time I slept with you."

She reached down to the river and splashed some foamy water at his face. "Take that…I didn't come upstream to spawn."

He wiped the foam from his cheek. "This fishing is serious business, Joyce. Let's go out in the water, and I'll show you how to net a fish." He waded out and glanced at her.

What hides behind her dark, mischievous eyes?

She sloshed out to the eddy whirling around his waders. "Oh, Father. Forgive me, for I know not what I do," she said, an impish grin breaking through. She bowed her head and looked down at the river grass waving in the stream. "Why do they call this river the Black? It's like crystal. Clear and icy."

"You're not getting out of this one." He raised the net and teased the wood rim under her chin.

She laughed. "It tickles. And it's cold."

He shook his head but kept the net on the tip of her chin. "Lesson one, page one. This little contraption is a fishing net. Its primary function is to net fish. When a fish is netted, it must be approached carefully, like this." He slowly submerged it into the current, the netting untangling and opening with the flow.

"This canyon is alive," she said, staring above at the swallows.

He jerked the net out of the water. "Pay attention."

"Do you miss it? And not the fish. The priesthood. You caught me. Or did I catch you? I'll never tell."

Dropping his net to hang on its elastic cord, he laid his hands on her shoulders. "We caught each other. But at times I want to shake you and hug you at the same time, and this is one of those times."

"Then hug me." She grasped his shirt collar and pulled down hard. "You were so handsome in your white, starched Roman collar, with that bald, shaved head. The way the girls looked at you. You were going to be my Yul Brynner."

"That's all over now. Let's don't let this fish—"

"How do you know that was the biggest brook trout you ever had on?"

"Let's forget about the trout. I'm sorry."

She let go and he slid his arms around her. She leaned in and they pressed their foreheads together and gazed into each other's eyes. She drew in close, pressed her lips against the corner of his mouth. Against the icy river, he felt her heat. When that became uncomfortable, they looked down at the greenish-yellow river grass rippling in the stream, its rhythm coupling them even closer.

For a long time, they were alone until startled by a swish and loud flapping. A hawk angled down directly above and dove with its wings held tight, piercing the water like an arrow and disappearing under the surface, then bursting up in a gush of spray with a large trout hooked in its talons. The trout thrashed about fiercely, slapping the river with its tail, splashing a shower of water. The hawk, twisting to shake off the droplets, let out a shrill scream and hovered momentarily just above water, pounding its drenched wings and rising, the trout clamped in its black claws.

Then all was calm. Swirling white foam and rippling waves lapped the shorelines and flowed downstream, the river recreating itself.

"Beautiful," Joyce said. She stood motionless, her eyes following the hawk.

"Flying wolves," he said, and they both squinted at the bird until it vanished over the trees.

Joyce remained fixed in the middle of the river, as if possessed.

Josh waded to the shore and walked along the bank downstream to the spot where Joyce had left her rod. He untangled her line, reeled in, and returned to stand next to her. She hadn't moved. He tapped her shoulder. She didn't respond. "Let's go to Ted's. He'll probably have dinner ready." He waded to the shore and climbed up the bank. "Let's go." Slowly she followed.

They trudged up the hill to his small pickup. He drove silently to Ted's on the Crocket Rapids Road, deeply rutted from early spring rains. On Monday evening, the Pigeon River Country State Forest was lonely, except for an occasional white-tailed deer or rare elk. Monday had always been his day off when he was a priest.

They passed through an orderly plantation of red pine; then through a dense stand of maples, the leafing trees encircling them in a dark tunnel. They exited the darkness and were cast into the glare of a setting sun and continued through a barren field recently leveled for its lumber with small sprouts of poplar breaking the ground.

"We're nearing the road to Saint Peter the Fisherman Mission Church," he said. "Pass it any minute now. Joyce…not there."

Joyce didn't reply. She raised her arm, which dangled outside the window, steadied her palm against the road wind, and lost herself in one of her trances, staring at the back of her hand as if saying *Peace* to the passing landscape. The image of the hawk rising with the trout hooked in its talons trailed off. But at the mention of Saint Peter the Fisherman Mission, drowned-out feelings of guilt resurfaced and possessed her.

RAPTURE RIVER

Hail to the spirit of wind with the palm of my hand the only reality of vision through me as wind and love of my spirit place is upon me as we drive toward the Mission chapel and the sacred ground of our first mystery not my mystery but our mystery of communion of spirit of body but now the haunting ghosts torturing me in my dream world with his guilt of our first union inside his church and he removing his white starched Roman collar and placing it in my hands and I charming him into our coupling and he now answering and in the sanctuary behind the altar saying no and walking out of the sanctuary and alongside the communion railing and he repeating no and I look up at him in my wanting with my hand holding and leading him down from the railing to the pews and his head shaking and saying no and coaxing him to the church foyer as face to face raising me and I digging my nails into the flesh of his shoulders drawing myself into him and he cradling me in his arms.

He stopped at the intersection of Tin Shanty Bridge and Elk Trail Roads. "Joyce, Joyce, wake up. Are you here? ... Not here."

He opened the CD compartment and took out John Denver's "Take Me Home, Country Roads," his mind trailing Joyce's into the passing woods.

Here, home had been the mission, Saint Peter the Fisherman Mission Catholic Church. He missed saying Mass for all the natives and weekend fishermen he had met over the last decade.

The church, on a bluff over the river, was decorated with stained glass windows and statues all related to fishing and waters—Christ walking on water, the whale giving up Jonah, Noah and his ark, St. Peter and his fishermen hauling in their nets. For centuries the hill itself had been claimed by the local Ojibwa to be holy ground. The local tribes were mainly Catholic but had held onto their sacred rituals—sweetgrass and jasmine smoldering in a smudge pot was their incense. The wild fragrance carried him into the spirit place, theirs and his—a realm in which nature and the soul became one, smothering out all borders. He longed for that time—his sermons flowing easily and spontaneously there.

Chapter 2

Josh drove off the gravel road up the two-track to Ted's cabin hidden from the main road by a stand of maples and backdropped by a clump of conifers, white and red pines. He was sitting on a pine stump under his kerosene lamp, skinning a woodchuck. Next to him sat his yellow Labrador Retriever Molly who came running up to Joyce as she opened the car door. Joyce knelt beside her, Molly licking her hand. "So good to see you, girl." The first time she smiled since the river.

They walked on a well-worn path over to Ted, who had on a blue baseball cap with "Peace" embroidered in yellow, his thick white hair rimming the edge like porcupine quills. Ted was eighty-nine and had worked in the steel mills of Gary, Indiana, for thirty years before retiring to northern Michigan when he was forty-nine. In forty years, he had created his own legend among the natives as chief scout of the Black River valley. Labor in the mills had muscled him into a hulk. Josh savored that memory when they had first crossed paths on a bend of the river while fishing, one year after he was ordained, ten years ago. On a stormy afternoon, foggy with the rain pelting down, they sat on the bank under a white cedar and shared their lives. And that chance meeting grew into an intimate friendship. When they parted, Ted had said that he'd give Josh his ordination into fly-fishing.

Ted looked up at Joyce. "You're tired."

"*Enh*." She nodded.

"Had a hard day on the river?"

She nodded again.

"I know what that man of yours is like on that river," he said, glancing at Josh. Then facing Joyce he continued, "But the river alone will own you, if you let it."

He picked up his deer knife on the stump and severed the pelt from the glistening furless body. "Now I have to flesh the hide." And he began to scrape the flesh and fat, absorbed in his work, totally oblivious of Joyce and Josh, concentrating on small sections and methodically moving onto the next, his massive muscular arms dwarfing the hide. His fingers, slimy with the grease of animal fat, were short and thick. Although the animal odor was strong, an encircling cluster of lilac bushes in full bloom snuffed out the smell, or at least made it more bearable.

Josh had always marveled at Ted's dexterity and how he could spin thread, feathers, and fur to create gorgeous flies, like the Fan-Winged Royal Coachman he had used that afternoon. But he had never seen him skin a woodchuck.

Ted eased off, stabbing the knife upright into the stump and stretching his fingers. "Can't waste God's gifts. This one I found along the road. A road-killed woodchuck that the crows were ready to feast on. I got there just as they were circling and beat them to it, or at least Molly did. She sniffed it out. For the crows it's a meal; for me, tail material for an Irresistible."

After scraping the pelt, he spread it out and nailed it to a pine board with the flesh side exposed.

"Joyce, could you please hand me the salt on that stump over there? When I sit down for too long, I have to tell my knees to get going. Sometimes I have to tell them two or three times."

Joyce handed him the salt. "The last time I skinned an animal was on the reservation, years ago."

"Do you miss it?"

"Sometimes terribly. I wish I were back there now."

"Home sweet home." Ted looked up at Josh. "And Father Joshua…Josh, could you take this furless critter and put it under that big oak by the side of the road? That's where we found it. The crows will finally get their meal too."

Josh picked up the woodchuck carcass by its hind leg, and Molly trailed at his heels.

"Molly, when are we going to have one of our long talks?" Molly looked up with her dark eyes, sensing his grief, her ears twitching. She brushed against his knee, and he knelt down beside her. "You know more about us than anyone. Don't you? I wish you could talk. I know you can think." Molly whined and nodded as if saying yes. He stood up, resumed walking. Why did Ted slip with Father? No one, not even Ted, could leave his priesthood alone, maybe force of habit, forgetfulness. Couldn't blame Ted. At one time his main love—that priesthood. He glanced back at his trail of boot prints in the soft dirt next to Molly's paw prints. Would they ever stop tracking him and trapping him in the cage of his past? He reached the gravel road, walked across, and laid the carcass under the oak, Molly sniffing at the remains of the roadkill she had come upon early morning.

When they returned, Ted was salting the pelt. He stood up slowly, picked up the board, and walked over to the shed, swinging from side to side like a black bear. "I'll leave this in the shed for five days to dry. I've got dinner ready. It's getting chilly out here." Ted had lived alone since his wife died ten years ago. He was proud of his living-off-the-land cooking. What he didn't catch or shoot, he foraged or grew himself.

"What's on the menu tonight?" Josh asked.

"Brook trout, morel mushrooms, a salad of watercress, tomatoes

I canned last year, and rhubarb pie. And sassafras tea… And Ottawa bread, Joyce… And the maple syrup I tapped this spring."

After Ted washed in the shed's tub, they followed him to the log cabin, Molly clinging to Joyce. Ted held onto the railing and wobbled up the two steps onto the porch and opened the door of slate pine bound with deer hide. They entered a semi-darkness. A fire flickered through the glass door of a wood burning stove in the middle of the room, crackling and bathing the rounded varnished logs and high ceiling with a soft mystic glow. Just inside on a pine stump was an albatross shell with the smoldering embers of sage. Wisps of smoke drifted up and rolled off the logs. They stopped, momentarily enchanted by this warm welcome.

"Watch your head," Ted said. "I've got enough feathers and pelts hanging from these overhead logs for a fly shop." Turkey and partridge wings, white deer tails, pieces of deer hide; brown, red, and black squirrel tails; a crow wing, a raccoon pelt, and a wood duck head and breast—all dangled by strings from two overhead log beams braided with sweetgrass, dispersing its woodsy fragrance.

Ted walked over to the far wall with Molly at his side, a polished path of unfinished floorboards creaking under his weight, while Joyce and Josh remained at the foyer. He lit a kerosene lamp hanging above a rough-hewn oak table set for three with ladder-back chairs in front of a large picture window overlooking the river. A stairway off to the left, next to the kitchen, led to a loft, where Joyce and Josh slept. On the right was Ted's room. Next to the dinner table was a plywood board lying on two sawhorses cluttered with fly-tying materials—a vise clamping a hook with an attached thread held taut by a wooden clothespin; peacock tails, glass bottles of wood duck breast feathers, vials of hackle varnish, rolls of fluorescent yarn, spools of yellow, brown, red, and black thread, and matchboxes filled with hooks.

RAPTURE RIVER

After dinner they sat looking out at the silvery rapids, sipping sassafras tea, a full moon reflecting off the river, while Molly lay on her mat under the sawhorse table.

"I have something to show you." Ted reached over to his fly-tying board, picked up a canning jar, unscrewed the cap, and took out a tuft of black fur. "This is from a black bear. One of the local Chippewa boys gave it to me. He cut it off a bear in Van Horn's swamp. There's a group of boys that call themselves The Bear Clan. Hear of it, Joyce?"

"No. Sounds like a secret society. Any girls belong?"

"Don't know. Well, to join you have to sneak up on a black bear and cut off a clump of his or her fur. Easier to get it from a male, I've been told. Females are more wary. Well, anyway, there's nine boys that belong to this clan, all Chippewa. Now the boy who gave me this, Jimmy Shananaquet, is on parole, on a tether. He was caught stealing a pair of scissors from one of those big chain store outfits… and besides, there was his drunken disorderly charge. It wasn't his first offense, but poverty breeds vice. With all that computer security, he got caught."

"He can sneak up on a black bear and get away but can't escape our man-made surveillance," Joyce said coldly.

Joyce had a master's degree in linguistics from the University of Michigan and went all the way through school on scholarships. She taught at the University for two years but decided she belonged with her own people. For the past three years, she had taught English and Ojibwa at the Peace Gathering, a minimum-security treatment facility for teenage boys. The facility could hold up to forty boys, most of whom were Native American.

Three years ago, Ted had met Joyce at the Peace Gathering. It was called a Gathering, not a minimum-security prison. The Peace

Gathering was located on the shores of Little Dipper Lake, a small spring-fed lake about the size of a football field. For the past ten years, Ted had given fly-fishing lessons on the lake. After the boys were released, he helped with their reintegration, taking them fly-fishing, allowing some to stay overnight at his cabin.

"Sad, isn't it," Ted said. "Something's out of joint. We prey upon each other. We're the most feared predator. Jimmy has to call his patrol officer when he wants to go out of his tether area. I've taken him fly-fishing."

He brushed the palm of his hand with the fur. Setting his elbow down, he held the tuft up over the middle of the table. The kerosene lamp overhead was beginning to flicker out and, in the dimness, he said, "They're holding another boy now, twenty years old, for the murder last week. I know he didn't do it."

"We read about it in the paper," Josh said.

"Not the gory details, though." Ted looked out the window. "I saw the corpse. I know the area by the river so well, like the back of my hand. They asked me to help search the area. Besides, the boy they're questioning is one of the boys I helped at the Gathering. A former inmate, Terry Benter. Know him, Joyce?"

"No. Before my time. Why him?"

"Because he's by the river over there a lot, fishing." He glanced at Joyce, who was staring at the black fur in his hands. "Mutilated. The murderer apparently jumped the victim sitting in his bulldozer having lunch and in the struggle bit his nose, or at least grabbed onto it with his teeth. The victim's nose was shredded into two globs of flesh hanging from his face. The murderer sliced his throat and attempted to scalp him. A poor try at scalping, I'm told. And this was near the site where some diesel fuel spilled and leaked into the river."

Oil and gas drilling had been in the Pigeon River Country for decades. It was well regulated and clean except for the occasional and accidental spill of diesel fuel or brine, which both Ted and Josh worried over. The salinity of the water could be affected and consequently the fish harmed.

Ted brushed the black fur against the table and looked at Joyce. "About blackness. How is your pet skunk?"

"Lady Slipper. I miss her. She's so affectionate. I'll see her this weekend at my grandmother's. It's my weekend at the blackjack table at the Michigan Sands. And, Ted, at class we've been reading *The Lord of the Rings,* and one of the boys said that the wizard Gandalf, that's Ted."

"I like that wizard part. Maybe they'll start listening to me. But never read it."

"I'll get you a copy. All we need is a ring, a gold ring."

"A ring we've got—a black ring, our new lord."

"And the gambling casino could probably fit in too—the land where the shadows lie."

Josh had questioned her gambling job, which she jokingly called a profession, but her only reply was that the extra money came in handy. It paid more than teaching and helped support her ninety-eight-year-old grandmother.

The kerosene lamp died out, and flashes of light from the fire in the wood stove skipped about the log walls, the silence broken only by the hiss and crackle of burning pine. The full moon illuminated the fur that Ted held. Ted looked at Joyce and Josh and then at the black bear fur.

Chapter 3

Clank. Clank. Clank. An apple, a pear, a lemon. Why couldn't he get three apples, or three pears, or three lemons? *I'm a loser. I'll always be a loser.* A rush surged up Dean Cassady's forearm muscles when he slammed down the lever. He avoided the new automatic push-button slot machines. No excitement in that. Dean shunned the poker room and the bingo hall and played in the blue haze of the smoking-allowed dome with its deafening chatter, throaty coughing, and screams of rapture. The voices that were always jabbering to him were silenced there.

But the Indian maidens. Ah, yes. The Indian maidens. They peered at him through their penetrating eyes of coal, picked up his ashes, served his rum and coke, and pranced away, their long black braids sparkling with beads swinging behind them as if they were inviting him to follow. *I have big gifts to offer you, boy. Come and enter the pleasure pit.*

The Indian gambling casino. Ah, yes, the Michigan Sands. Here at the Michigan Sands, he was treated very politely as he threw away his money—the big checks the oil company squandered throughout the county, bribing good country people, creating the illusion of woodland wealth.

No oil on his five little acres with his trailer propped smack in the middle. But on quiet summer nights he'd wake up, startled by the distant, faint cranking of an oil rig and the odor of spilled diesel fuel. And he worried that they were sucking oil from under his trailer through one of their horizontal pipes, miles away. His well water wasn't contaminated—yet—but if it were he'd have a damage claim and his income could spike.

Restless in the middle of a humid summer night, he'd step outside his trailer nude and circle it again and again, his bare feet cushioned by the soft white pine needles that had built up over the years. In his hand, he clenched the jackknife his father had given him on his twelfth birthday. He'd stop, kneel, and lower his head to the ground, sniffing like a hound dog. Crawling on all fours he'd pause when he reached a sweet spot, paw the packed needles away, and set his ear against the dirt to hear the gushing of oil through pipes deep under. And he'd see it swirling through rings of black gold. After a few minutes he'd stand and spit upon the bare spot, and he'd watch his spittle fizz up from the fire deep under, reeking of its oily scent. Then rising above the depths of middle earth, he was aroused by the faint rippling of the river, just over the hill, and seduced again into a trance. He'd tighten his grip on his jackknife and could see his father beside him fly-fishing the river when he was a little boy. He heard the comfort of his voice. "Cast next to that log by the bank, Dean. There's a big one feeding there." And recalled the time he was lost along the river, the echo of his father calling out— "Dean, Dean." And then those moments of bliss would vanish.

But at the casino tonight, all night would be his lucky night. Tonight was his one-week anniversary. Dean Cassady would celebrate the salvation of the river and his own damnation.

He walked coolly up to the token counter, cashed a fifty-dollar bill for fifty one-dollar gambling tokens. The cashier slid five neat columns of coins under the window bars.

"Good luck," she said, "and I like your black Michigan Sands T-shirt, Dean. Shows off your muscles. And when are you getting a haircut? You can tie it back with an all-gold barrette with tonight's winnings."

"Why, thank you, Kathy." Dean smiled and stared at her shiny black eye. "Is Joyce at the blackjack table tonight?"

Looking down at the tokens, she said, "You mean Soar with Red-Tailed Hawks? Not tonight."

"Soar with Red Tails," Dean said.

"I grew up with Joyce," Kathy said.

"I never knew her Indian name," Dean said. "It fits her. She's probably with that squeeze priest of hers. Hear about it?"

"Everybody has. The whisper spreads fast around these parts. What else is there?"

Dean nodded. He picked up a red plastic bucket, placed the lid under the counter edge, and swiped the five stacks into it. He untied the thongs to the deerskin pouch strapped to his belt, poured the coins in, and reset the bucket on the shelf. He stepped over to the bar, placed two tokens down, and ordered a rum and coke. Drink in hand, he wandered through the sparse night crowd, tokens jingling on the swinging pouch, not a soul acknowledging him, all engrossed in their own slot machines. He walked through pine doors into the smoking dome and picked a Marlboro and lighter from his shirt pocket, lit the cigarette, took a deep drag, and stood there peering through the blue haze. His slot machine was vacant, third one from the aisle on the third row. He stepped over, sat down, and placed his drink in the holder. Two machines over, the white-haired fat lady was sliding her credit card into the slot. She smiled and he nodded. They had never passed words. He played all night, refilling his pouch and drink three times.

"It's getting close to closing time, Mr. Cassady," the security guard said. "We've only got three hours to tidy up and reopen."

"Man, I've had another cool night. Thank you."

With no outside light and no clock, he guessed it was near dawn. He had won some but lost more. He walked up to the cashier counter, picked up a moist towelette, tore open the wrapper, wiped the metallic black from his fingers, and inhaled the lemony scent.

"Any luck?" the cashier asked.

He shrugged and stared at her single shiny black eye.

He passed through the casino's gilded entrance held by the doorman, who said, "Good evening, Mr. Cassady. Or is it morning?"

He nodded and walked out into a false dawn, a full moon playing tricks with light. He unlocked his small pickup. The clock said 5:00, an hour before sunrise. He decided to take the long way home on unpaved backroads. After an hour of driving, he flipped down his visor to block the sun's glare. Roosting birds were awakening and beginning their morning feed.

"Damn you, you black bastard." He slammed on the brakes to avoid the crow, but it splattered over his windshield. He stopped, jumped out, ripped some leaves from a sassafras tree, and wiped at the blood on the glass.

He saw the crow on the side of the road, walked to it, knelt down, touched the wet, warm breast, and looked around. The crows had scattered, but a few remained under an oak.

"Bold critters. Looks like...feeding on a road-killed woodchuck."

Chapter 4

Josh stood by the hexagonal window in the loft. On the ground around Ted's bird feeder, mourning doves were breaking their night fast, pecking at the seeds.

Joyce was awakening. She turned over and pulled the quilt up to her chin. "I had that dream again. The same one. But this time it was even scarier. They're becoming more vivid and in color now. There was—"

"I don't want to hear about it. Ted's putting something together au natural for breakfast. What that odor is, I don't know, but it smells tasty. See you downstairs."

Holding onto the loft railing, he stepped down the stairs, drawing aside the curtain of fur and feathers.

Ted was bent over his gas stove. He had on a long white apron over his red chamois shirt and khaki pants. "Get Joyce up," he said. "We have some *bebaabgaanh* for breakfast."

"Get up, Joyce, we have some *beb* whatever for breakfast."

"Pancakes with my maple syrup, *bebaabgaanh*," Ted said.

"That's it."

"Not all. We have brook trout for bacon. I caught a sixteen-inch brook trout between Tin Shanty Bridge and McKinnan's Bend yesterday morning."

Josh walked over to the window. Wisps of vapor curled off the river. Off to the side, the black tarred roof and tin smokestack of Ted's sugar shack poked out of a clump of leafing maples. "How was the maple syrup harvest this year?"

"Two boys from the Peace Gathering helped me tap the trees, but I needed four boys to boil it down. The sap flowed till the end of March."

"The best year you ever had?" Josh asked.

"Not quite. The year Lake Superior froze over, '93 or '94. That year would be hard to beat. How are the girls lately? Any challenges?"

"Always." Josh had a master's degree in sociology. After quitting the priesthood he had worked in Social Services, specializing in counseling divorced and unmarried mothers who, at times, were reduced to beggars, supporting themselves on a waitress's income, some desperate enough to sell themselves.

Joyce walked down the stairs wrapped in a patch quilt and plunked down in a ladderback chair set at the table. "Coffee, please." Her hair was tied in a black bun on the top of her head with a rubber band, a few black strands uncurling and falling over her ears.

After breakfast they lingered at the table, sipping coffee and savoring the aftertaste of Ted's maple syrup.

"This is virgin syrup," Ted said. "No additives, no preservatives. That's why it stays with you so long."

"Unless I get some more rest, I won't be good for fishing when the hatches are on this afternoon," Joyce said. "There will be a hatch on this afternoon, Ted?"

"I'm expecting a March Brown hatch after it warms up, any time this afternoon. Maybe a Pale Evening Dun hatch. There isn't a Pale Morning Dun, *Ephemerella infrequens*, out there now, too early." Ted stared out the window and smiled. "Adoptiva, Bivisible, Light Cahill, Gold-Ribbed Hare's Ear, Black-Nosed Dace, Blue-Winged Olive. The poetry of fly-fishing."

After breakfast Joyce retired to the loft. Ted and Josh put on their coats, went out the door, walked on the two-track to the gravel road, and began their short hike to Johnson's grave on the bluff overlooking the Black River Valley. Molly ran ahead to sniff out the discarded carcass. They had taken this route many times together.

Crows were feeding on the woodchuck Josh had placed under the oak last evening. They scattered but a few held their ground, tearing at the flesh until Molly closed in. With his walking stick Ted flipped over a dead crow. "Someone probably hit it this morning. Look at those deep skid marks. That's braking hard."

They continued to Johnson's grave. Johnson was a state conservationist who dedicated his life to developing and preserving the Black River Valley. The area was eventually named the Pigeon River Country State Forest.

When they reached the knoll, Ted sat down on a boulder next to the gravestone, a bronze plaque imbedded in a rock heralding that a human soul hovered over this valley.

"He won't mind me sitting here," Ted said. "Soon I'll probably meet him here again when I cross over to the other side of paradise, the happy hunting ground. We met once, the first year I came up here, when I was sixteen. Didn't know who I was meeting then."

Josh leaned against the lone pine near the edge over the valley, Molly at his side. Steep slopes dense with red pine abruptly ended in a vaporous marsh that hugged the river. Solar heat was beginning to disperse the cold fog. Little black specks were whirling around cattails, red-winged blackbirds hot into their spring dominance rituals.

"There's a legend about red-winged blackbirds," Josh said, "and how they got their red wings. When Christ was on the cross, a red-winged blackbird alighted on the crown of thorns and plucked them out. A squirt of blood wetted its wings and created in God's eyes a red-winged blackbird. Such a stark contrast with its blackness. And you wonder—that had to be created, not just happen, and maybe by that miracle."

"Beautiful. They'll be active today. It's getting warm. They got here about the middle of April, a little early this year. All the way from Georgia. By the first of May, the males had collected their mates. So…what is it, Josh?"

"What's what?"

"When you came downstairs this morning, I saw it in your eyes."

Josh walked over to the edge of the bluff.

Ted leaned over and petted Molly. "You can't run away from it. Sometimes it's best to tell it out. Get rid of it. Off your chest. Face up to it. And what is confession? Something sacred. A sacrament."

Josh stared into the valley, his back toward Ted. "It's about a dream. Joyce's dream. She had it again last night. Well…in her dream…"

"Get on. Turn around now. You aren't talking to the river. Well, the river, she's listening anyway."

"In her dream we were making love—I was above her. I didn't have a face. I was headless."

Ted looked off over the horizon. The long shadows from the rising sun over the opposite bank cast a dark pall over the river. "That's not a dream. That's a nightmare. And what does Joyce say about this…dream?"

"She said she had it again last night."

"Probably why she didn't get much sleep last night. She was haggard this morning."

Ted touched the plaque with his fingertips. "It's still cold." He looked up at Josh. "With no face? No identity. Are you sure it's you? Women can be kind of indirect at times. You might say devious."

Josh stomped over to the boulder. "I…"

"Now, now, now. Take it easy. I'm sure it's you. That girl loves you and it's not just physical. A man doesn't live for eighty-nine years, sixty of them with one woman, and raise four girls without knowing what—"

"But not Joyce. There's a thing about Joyce. Sometimes I think she's two people. She has this playful, saucy personality and this serious, analytical one."

"I've seen this in her. Both of you are two. She's trying to pull her white, educated teacher and her Native American instincts together. And she sees you as two. You're cut off from yourself. No courtship ever worked its way out smooth in a perfect world. Look what we've got—murder, a damaged river, and what more will jump out of the bushes. It's better being an animal like Molly, but I'd guess she has hers. You'll make it."

Molly whined.

Josh touched the plaque. "It's been difficult. I especially loved the priesthood up here."

"First time I heard you say that word in a long time."

His eyes turning red, Josh said, "I wonder how much salt spilled onto this rock over the last fifty years."

"Just being up here will do it. Nature. That red-winged blackbird story almost did it to me."

Josh sat down on the rock. He stared into the valley at the river. The river was his social worker, his own psychiatrist, his healer. He had participated in, actually had performed healing ceremonies with vague results. The eyes of the participants imploringly looking up as they knelt and he anointed their foreheads with the blessed oil. And although he didn't believe in miracles, he accepted the healing powers of the natural world. Those moments in the river when he became totally immersed in the process of fly-fishing, when

he had no thoughts, and his world was the flow of water and a floating fly. And time, time kept but not kept, as it swept by until the plaque warmed from the sun.

Ted braced himself up with his walking stick. "Old hickory, light, strong, and it's carried me for ten years. And that's a lot of hefting up."

As they walked the path to the road, they heard the crackle of tires on gravel. They waited in the tall grass by the side of the road to let the vehicle pass. As it reached the crest of the hill, Ted waved and smiled. Ted's best friend, Ken O'Madden, the Elk County sheriff, was behind the wheel of his patrol vehicle.

He pulled over to the side and rolled down his window. Ted stepped over to the car and they shook hands. Josh had always wondered who would fare best in an arm-wrestling contest, although Ted was thirty years his senior. Sheriff Mad, as he was known throughout the county, was everybody's friend. But Josh saw through a carefree, jolly front that camouflaged a sensitive butterfly heart. His wife had succumbed to a long battle with cancer a few years ago. Josh had met her once on one of the rare occasions when they attended Mass together.

"The mad Irishman," Ted said. "Good to see you. How's business?"

"It gets better by the minute. Besides the murder, I had an exciting evening… Hey, Josh!"

"Come on out and let's sit down and talk about it," Josh said.

Ken lifted himself out of his patrol car, his belly hanging over his black belt like an extra appendage. He took his trooper hat off, slung it through the window onto the seat, and ran his hands through his thick reddish gray hair. "They can shove this protocol crap." He petted Molly. "I was as golden as you are, long ago, lady."

They walked back to the boulder. Ted and Ken sat down on the boulder, and Josh stood off to the side with Molly.

"So, business is good?" Ted asked.

"It was Jedidiah Lewis again, last night."

"I knew Lewis, Jedidiah Lewis, from the mission church. He's a very spiritual man," Josh said. "Actually, Jedidiah is Hebrew for 'Beloved of the Lord.'"

"Lot of stories about Lewis. He was playing soldier last night—never could get over Vietnam. He was running down the interstate, completely naked, streaking. Half drunk, of course. He stuck to the median grass mainly but every once in a while dodged in and out of the traffic lanes, on both sides."

"I heard he was cured," Ted said.

"For a year or so. He regresses. He's been through AA and therapy at the VA. They always send me to pick him up. When I drove up and got out, he took the big stick he was carrying, put it on his shoulder like a rifle, stood at attention, and said, 'Mission accomplished, Captain.'"

Ted and Josh shook their heads.

"Hell. If I said, 'There's more enemy out there, soldier, and don't return until you get them all,' he probably would have kept on running. So, I bundled him up in some blankets and took him in. Could have died of exposure."

"How long has he been doing this?" Josh asked.

"Off and on for a few years," Ken said. "Thought it was all over. But you never know. Couple of years ago someone at headquarters took his photo and hung it up on our bulletin board list of most loved inmates. But the girls always commented on his lean, muscular physique; must be over six feet and ties his two black braids together with a leather thong laced with bear claws."

"Sad," Josh said.

"Yeah, it is. Someone at the travel bureau even said that Lewis was good for business, a tourist attraction. Maybe we should advertise—Come see the wild aboriginal red man run down the freeway chasing the elusive fang-toothed prehistoric wolf." Ken picked up Ted's cane, which had slid off the rock, and handed it to him.

"So, what brought you up this way?" Ted asked.

"I'm looking for Coop. I haven't talked to him yet about the murder. I was going to stop by your place to see if you knew his whereabouts."

"I haven't seen him, but one of the boys told me he saw Coop when he was in Van Horn's swamp stalking a bear. So, he made it through the winter again."

"Never saw him myself, but I heard vague stories from my former parishioners at the mission about a hermit," Josh said.

"Chicken Coop," Ted said, gripping his cane with both hands. "Chicken Coop goes back to the other war, my war, the Korean War. He must be close to a hundred years old, tall, thin, and wiry. He lives in a shack, a converted chicken coop, with only a woodstove for heat. No running water. After the war he couldn't adjust. Shell shock. Now they call it stress disorder."

Ted tapped his cane against the rock. "He's not all there, drifts in and out. He might know something and he might not. Depends on when you catch him. He's probably at his shack this morning after roaming around early on. Gets up before dawn to catch his breakfast. You'll probably smell him before you see him."

"Another thing about the murder," Ken said. "The body was on federal land. Already I've talked to a federal marshal. If we get the murderer, they want to try him in U.S. District Court, not the Elk County Circuit Court. Then they could go for the death penalty. Just another headache for me, dealing with these federal people. If you want to call them people human beings. But then, I can go along with the death penalty. But Michigan doesn't."

"The death penalty," Josh said.

"You frown. Don't believe in it?"

"No."

"Well, in a way," the sheriff rubbed his chin, "they do have jurisdiction over the trees and the river, but over the people…I don't know. They call themselves the landowners and say they're the sheriff now, taking over my job. But there's that marriage between the oil companies and the federal government. There'll never be a divorce there…not if that land is pregnant with gas."

Josh looked down over the river. "But already there have been several miscarriages, accidental spills."

Chapter 5

Mobbing, the red-winged blackbirds had gathered into an attack flock. They surrounded a red-tailed hawk as it hovered high over the river. Diving methodically at the hawk, they pecked at its wings and back, the hawk falling in midair, flapping its wings awkwardly to regain its glide on the air currents.

Dean looked above through the open canopy over the river at the same territorial fight that he was the master of. But he would not just peck and torment the oil company. He would butcher them away.

He had been awake, excited, and moving for twenty-four hours and he loved it. He was on river time now, clocked by the sun and the instinctive patterns of birds, mammals, mayflies, and trout. But he knew he would give in, crash, lie down on the riverbank grass after he had fly-fished all day.

He stood in midstream up to his waist in the slow, deep water of Van Horn's swamp. The river here was the color of tea, from the cedar trees that hugged the banks and held the black earth firmly in their gnarly roots. All was quiet until a slight breeze picked up and rattled the leaves of a stand of poplar, the wind hitting him directly in his face. Through the trees he saw a blackness. A trout struck his fly. He missed, the trout not hooked, his eyes fixed on the blackness moving in the poplars. Had to be a black bear.

He froze, until the cold blade of a knife pressed against his lips.

Dean looked down at the icy steel and then slowly, carefully turned his head to the side. Standing beside him was Billy Blackhawk, hunting knife in hand. Billy flattened the blade over Dean's lips and whispered, "Shhh," and smiled. He lifted the blade from Dean's mouth and secured it in the sheath around his neck.

Dean nodded.

Billy slowly treaded his way to the shore and climbed the bank by grasping the cedar roots. He rested against a cedar tree and smiled again at Dean. He took off his hiking boots, set them by the tree, and slipped on his moccasins that had hung around his neck. His blue jeans and denim shirt clung to his lithe frame. He crouched, peeked around the tree at the black bear, and began his stalk.

When he reached the clump of poplars, he lay face down in the grass. His heart pounded against the earth. Small beads of his sweat trickled down upon the reeds of grass, poled, and soaked the dark soil under his nose. He slowly raised his head. The bear had moved closer, only ten feet away, her rich rump of black fur directly in front of him. She looked at her two cubs playing in the leaves. He crawled around the side opposite the cubs, inching along. He could smell her foul breath from the grubs she was feeding on. He knelt at her rump with his knife raised. As his knife touched the fur, a shrill squeal stopped him. He turned and saw the blue eyes of the third cub. The bear swung around and clawed at Billy's head. He spun away, sprang up, and ran, all in one instantaneous motion. The bear lunged at his black head again, crashing after him through the trees.

Billy felt her hot breath as he dove off the bank between two cedars and splashed into the deep pool of Kiss-Ass bend. He twisted under water, swam back to the caverns under the bank, and surfaced there, his knife clenched in his teeth. Holding onto the lacework of cedar roots, he could hear her heavy breathing above.

She stands between two cedars on her hind legs. She snarls and sniffs, piercing the air with her nose, picking up the lingering stench of man's fear. She looks down upon the water, her swamp, her home. She glances at the three cubs. The male had warned her. She growls, calls the two girls. They squeal, and the male follows.

An hour after Billy's stalk, the swamp settled back into its own life—the squirrels began to chatter, and the red-winged blackbirds returned to their nests along the river.

From the river Dean had seen the blackness moving in the distance and heard the crashing. Then he saw nothing. A breeze picked up again and rattled the leaves of poplars. Above there were no crows or vultures—the non-violent rhythms of nature had returned.

He wondered if Billy had finally won his tuft of fur. On the bank next to the cedar lay Billy's hiking boots. Dean waded to the bank, grasped the roots, and hefted himself up. He picked up Billy's boots and peered past the cedars. All was quiet. Dean tied the laces together and hung the boots over his shoulder

"I'll see Billy in Onaway at The Whisper. What in the hell went on at Kiss-Ass bend, Blackhawk?" His voice an off note against the music of the swamp.

Chapter 6

"Kirtland's warbler. Hear it," Ted said. "There's only a few that nest in the jack pine clump here. Heard them yesterday when I caught that brook trout we had for breakfast this morning."

They sat in Ted's jeep, the engine off. Ted had driven to Van Horn's swamp, Josh in the front and Joyce in the back with Molly. He had parked on a ridge of jack pine above the cedar swamp. Josh had been here before with Ted, but this was Joyce's first time. Warblers had nested in this spot for hundreds of years, migrating from the Bahamas to mate in the spring and in the fall flying back to their warm winter home. Ted had trained Molly to hold back from their nests.

"I'll go downstream," Ted said.

Ted opened his door and stepped out of the jeep. Molly sprung out first, followed by Josh and Joyce.

A quickness took possession of Ted whenever he was near the river, and Josh always enjoyed Ted's enthusiasm. He hoped it was contagious and that he'd catch it. He could shed thirty years in thirty minutes. His excitement was enhanced by Molly, who always accompanied him along the river, but he had trained her not to disturb his fishing. She stood calmly on the bank as he waded, watching over and guarding her master. She was hefty for a female Labrador, weighing eighty-five pounds. In no time he had his waders on and began to walk on the path to the river.

Joyce and Josh sat on a log by a stone firepit.

Ted stopped and walked back to the jeep, Molly with him. "Forgot my walking stick," he said. "Need that. Almost slipped on some clay yesterday."

His stick lay by the firepit. Josh picked it up and handed it to him. "We'll be getting ready in a bit."

Ted nodded. He looked at Josh and then at Joyce. His dark brown eyes possessed a penetrating sadness, as if he yearned to say something but couldn't.

He turned and walked down the path to the river, flipping his cane in a wide arc.

They watched him until he faded into the cedar swamp.

Joyce picked up a stone and tossed it at the rocks around the firepit. "Let's build a fire. I'm too worn out to fish."

"Worn out?"

"You would be too."

"Why?"

"You know why."

"Over that nightmare?"

"Yes."

"I told Ted."

"I know. You're frightened now."

"Who wouldn't be. Dreams foretell. Look at the dreams of Joseph and his Angel—"

"Don't expect another virgin birth."

Josh stood up and walked around the firepit. "You're pregnant?"

She looked up, then turned her gaze into the swamp. "*Gnimaa.* Maybe."

"Maybe."

"*Enh.* Yes. Maybe."

"Are you happy?"

"Are you? It's not the you and me. It's the us. The we. And should I call it the it I'm worried about. Our coupling and my dream. Let's build a fire." She rearranged the remnants of half-burnt kindling twigs scattered around the pit.

Maybe, maybe, maybe I'm pregnant from the wisdom words of my grandmother who birthed thirteen children but two stillborn only their spirits alive and telling me this is the great spirit's way and we are not given to understanding and her anger at our past and wanting more males hunting and warring and an unwanted female infant placed in the crook of a tree to feed the crows and eagles so her spirit flies and I surviving because I am cultured with bachelor and master's degrees that mask my nomadic instincts forcing me to paved streets and soaring concrete glass and plastic buildings that scrape the sky and ascend higher and higher into the dirt of our own plastic air and always wanting more and not clinging to the great spirits gifting of the circle of life.

Josh gathered dried jack pine branches, shying away from the trees where warblers would be nesting. They built their nests on the ground under immature jack pines, less than six feet in height. The lower branches drooped onto the ground and spread into the grass and sandy soil, the gnarly limbs penning around their eggs, a fortress against predators.

Josh picked up Joyce's blanket in the jeep and walked back to the firepit. She was gathering more twigs for kindling. She piled them in the center of the pit and then sat down on the log.

Josh handed her the blanket and settled the branches over the kindling sticks. He walked back to Ted's jeep and picked up some old newspapers on the floorboards and read the headlines— "Diesel Fuel Spill Near Black River."

He walked back to the fire, knelt down, and balled up the paper around the kindling wood, took a pack of matches from his breast pocket, struck one, and lit the newspapers.

He sat down on the log next to Joyce.

They stared at the fire, spreading and feeding upon itself, born again and again, the branches crackling and falling into its core, the twigs vanishing into smoke and heat, the popping sap oozing.

She picked up a twig and flipped it in the fire. "You could begin counseling me. This would be my first appointment."

"That's the most difficult one," Josh said. "We'd have to cross over some treacherous rapids."

"But you could carry me."

"Yes, I know I could."

"But not right now. I'm not ready yet. In our little office of the fire. Let's dream the fire."

"Dream the fire?"

"*Enh*. Yes."

"How?"

"Simply stare at the flames. Let them take you. There's an expression in Swahili, the lingua franca of eastern Africa. The Masai tribes, another conquered people, have an expression that has no literal translation. When one sits around the fire and is caught up in it, one is 'dreaming the fire.'"

"Dream the fire," Josh said. "Maybe the fire could burn the darkest dreams away."

"Why not?" Joyce wrapped the blanket around her. She lay down and curled up with her back against the log. "I'm so tired."

"Go to sleep."

"I will. Good night."

"Good night."

Josh sat on the log and looked beyond the haze and heat of the fire. The swamp scintillated in the distance on this screen of fire. Trunks of cedar trees shimmered into the deepening shadows as the late horizontal rays of sun bent into the cooling vapors of swamp water, creating a mirage as if viewing this scene through a glass of running water. And on this screen—Ted wading, casting effortlessly toward the grassy banks, the mayflies dipping down onto the silvery surface, falling like snowflakes, and the brook trout rising and dimpling the surface with perfect concentric rings, while the swamp waters flowed and merged into a faraway black hole.

Josh shook his head to clear his mind of this vaporous trance and looked at Joyce. She was sound asleep. What dreams was she flowing into?

He lay down with his back against the log and dreamt the fire.

The fire kindled his dream and in it Joyce and Josh were riding on the back of a white dove, facing each other, their legs astraddle, buried in white fluff, flying high up over the swamp, the air cool and refreshing, the dove soaring. Joyce levitated above the soft down and hovered over Josh. They embraced and lingered in an endless orgiastic high, their eyes swimming into each other's pleasure. They could not only see each other but the whole of everything below, as if their world had merged into one. Under was a lacework of rivulets, each branch with its own distinct color, all coursing and flowing into the main river. But the red, white, blue, green, and yellow stream did not coalesce into one color. After joining the main river, each rivulet had its own level, and all colors flowed separately, but they saw each color and all colors at the same time. This current of rainbows cascaded into foamy rapids, and the many-hued branches splashed against giant whitewashed boulders, releasing a kaleidoscope of spray. Beyond, this splendor blended into an effervescent, sparkling lake banked by giant, crystalline cedars.

Josh was awakened from his dream by the call of a whip-poor-will. Nine o'clock. He had slept three hours. What other dreams had he dreamed? He raised his head from the log and stood up. Darkness. The only light from the coals of the spent fire. A starless sky foreshadowed an advancing cold front and rain.

Off in the distance toward the south, he saw a flashlight wobbling from side to side, occasionally stopping and continuing. Ted walking back on the trail.

Joyce was waking up. She pointed toward the swamp. "That flashlight is moving awful fast through the swamp," she said.

She was looking north. There was a flashlight advancing rapidly, almost in a straight line, occasionally bobbing up, probably over a log, as if its carrier were determined to get somewhere fast.

"That's not Ted," Josh said. "Ted's coming up from the river over there, moving slowly with Molly. Must be another fisherman. I wonder if they met on the river."

"They're getting farther apart."

"And how far along—"

"Am I."

"Yes. How many months?"

"One."

"Did you see a doctor?"

"No. I told my grandmother how I felt last weekend. She had thirteen children. She said yes I am."

Josh sat down next to her and pulled the blanket around them. "Let's celebrate."

She smiled. "Here."

"Why not?"

They curled up under the blanket by the dying embers.

"*Nswi*. Three of us now. Together."

Chapter 7

Sheriff O'Madden hit his brakes hard and veered to the right, his patrol car skidding on the wet pavement onto the grassy shoulder. He stopped. His bright lights angled into the scrub oaks. Through the rhythmic sloshing of his windshield wipers, he saw the white tail bob into the darkness. "Damn. One of these days my luck will run out and I'll hit one."

He pulled back onto the blacktop and drove down the road to The Whisper, an old farmhouse remodeled into a restaurant that had become a hub of gossip. He parked his vehicle, stepped out, walked up the porch steps, and opened the hundred-year-old door.

He stood in the foyer. Billy Blackhawk sat in a booth in the far corner. He waved to the sheriff.

He walked over, sat down opposite Billy, and nodded to the waitress, Gretchen. She came to their table to take his order.

"So what's the latest buzz, Gretchen?"

"Sheriff Mad. You come here to gossip or to eat?" She poured his coffee.

"Both. And to see you." He stood up, leaned over, and whispered in her ear. "I like the reddish tint in your hair. You look ravishing this morning."

"Hands, hands, hands, Sheriff Mad. And better watch that tongue."

"That was just a tap."

"More like a pinch. But not quite a grab." She laughed. "What's for breakfast."

"Usual. But make it six eggs over easy, six sausage, six flapjacks, and six wheat toast. Six, six, six, and six. That will make it easy for you. To hell with this damn diet. I'll outlive my doctor."

Gretchen returned to the kitchen with his order.

"I'm celebrating anyway, Billy. I found Coop."

"How's Coop?" Billy asked as he picked up a piece of bacon and rolled it in his egg yolk.

"I smelled him before I saw him. But since when is he mute? I think he heard me. He just nods his head. Doesn't answer."

"Coop's losing it slowly."

"He handed me this." The sheriff took a gambling token out of his pocket and laid it on the table. A thick plastic coin. On one side, an eagle in flight against a blue sky with the inscription Soaring Eagle Casino. On the other side, $1.00.

Billy picked up the coin. "I gambled yesterday and lost."

"How much?"

"A hair."

"A hair?"

"Yeah. Bear's hair." Billy told him about his escape from the bear and passing Dean on the river. He flipped the coin. It landed on the table eagle-side up. "She's a loud eater. Feeding on grubs. And the foulest breath."

"As loud as Coop?" the sheriff said. "I took Coop six hamburgers, and he ate them all, at one sitting. Sounds like a cement mixer. Burps like a foghorn."

Gretchen served Sheriff Mad his breakfast. He ate intensely, wiping his plate with his last piece of wheat bread.

He sat back and looked up at the entrance. Dean stood in the foyer, holding a pair of hiking boots over his head.

"You forgot these, Billy," Dean said. He walked over to their booth, pulled a chair over, and sat down, setting the boots on the floor. "Mind if I join you? I guess you don't mind since I'm already sat down. Howdy, Sheriff."

The sheriff nodded.

"What in hell went on at Kiss-Ass Bend?" Dean asked Billy.

Billy told him.

Dean picked up the gambling token. "Whose gambling token?"

"Mine," Sheriff Mad said. "A friend gave it to me. Said it was good luck."

Billy looked up at the sheriff.

"So what have you been up to lately?" the sheriff asked Dean.

"Walking to and fro upon the earth and in the rivers. Fishing. Last night I passed Ted. I got out of the river and walked around downstream. He didn't see me, but I didn't disturb his fishing."

"Any luck?"

"No. But today I'll be searching for rattlesnakes. Preacher Jacob wants some local snakes in his Sunday services at Holiness Tabernacle Church."

"Local snakes?" the sheriff asked. "I thought we had more than enough local snakes."

Dean tapped the coin on the table. "Reverend Jacob will bring up a couple of rattlesnakes and cottonmouths from Tennessee. Big snakes down there. He's visiting his stepdaughter up here, starting his mission church. We ain't got a full-time minister yet, but we'll be gettin' one. The reverend tries to get up here three weeks a month for services. He says God has called upon him to spread the Signs Followers."

The sheriff looked at Billy and then at Dean. "You know that it's against the law to kill a massasauga rattler. They're protected."

"Us serpent handlers don't kill snakes. We protect them. We pet them. They love it. Go limp in our hands. Attend the service tomorrow, Sheriff."

"It's not for me."

"You don't have to handle the snakes. Only if you're called upon by the Lord. The Spirit will anoint you, and only you'll know if you've been called. I've seen people come to our church the first time and no way were they going to handle snakes, and all of a sudden, they are anointed by the Spirit and standing in front of the congregation with a pile of snakes in their hands."

The sheriff shook his head. "I read in the paper where a rattler killed an eighty-five-pound black Labrador."

"The Lord don't anoint no dogs." Dean looked at the sheriff, placed the coin on the table, and stood up. He glanced out the window. "It's starting to clear. I better get out there. The snakes will be on the feed."

"Thanks for the boots," Billy said.

"My pleasure."

The sheriff picked up the plastic token, clinked it against his coffee cup, and watched Dean walk out of The Whisper. "He looks like a snake charmer."

Billy nodded.

Chapter 8

Holy Tabernacle Church was a quarter mile off the freeway down a two-track. A sign of white pine nailed to an oak tree was carved with "The Signs Followers." Halfway to the church the trail dipped down, crossed over the culvert on Danaher Creek, then rose again to a hill that overlooked an open field. In the middle of that field was an abandoned one-room schoolhouse, freshly painted white. The bell tower housed a new bell. There was a portable green toilet off to the side. This Sunday morning eight vehicles were parked on the grass—four rusted-out cars and four pickup trucks with their beds overfilled with pine logs.

Dean Cassady drove down the hill and parked his pickup on the grass next to the other vehicles. He stepped down onto the grass, slammed the door, and walked around to the back of his pickup. He lifted a large burlap sack out of the bed. A thick rope knotted the opening. He held the sack off to the side and walked on the dirt path up to the church, clutching onto a railing as he ascended two shaky stairs. He opened the door and entered.

There were a dozen parishioners seated on makeshift pine pews. Next to the door a grizzly-bearded man holding a guitar nodded and smiled at Dean. Dean nodded back. Still holding the sack off to the side, he walked up the aisle to the tabernacle table. Dean set the sack down next to two others. As the bag collapsed upon itself, a sharp rattle and hiss pierced the stillness, and the sack began to whip itself around, thrashing on the floor.

Dean slowly walked to the back of the church and sat down.

Reverend Jacob was standing behind the church on a well-worn trail. He was a tall, lanky man with a thick head of white hair and penetrating blue eyes. He had on black corduroy pants and a black cotton shirt with a white tie.

He knelt on both knees and looked up at the sky, his arms outstretched as if he were reaching for and grasping something unseen. He stood up and paced back and forth on the path and began to speak in tongues, babbling sacred truths to an unknown. He stomped on the path, hitting the ground firmly with each step, the heels of his black cowboy boots digging into the moist earth. He quickened his stride from one side of the church to the other and then stopped suddenly. He remained stone rigid, a statue cast in black. Within a few minutes his arms and legs began to quiver, then shake, and in a rising crescendo his whole body flung into violent spasms. He was brought down to his knees and thrown upon the earth; his face pressed against the ground. The tremors stopped as suddenly as they had begun. He arose slowly and standing straight, he looked up at the passing white clouds through his bloodshot eyes and said, "Thank You, Lord."

He walked around the church to the entrance.

Grasping the wrought-iron handle, he opened the door and lingered there looking over this morning's assemblage—twelve.

RAPTURE RIVER

"That's all I need." Four men and eight women—country people. Fishermen, carpenters, loggers, homemakers—the salt of the earth. Dressed in their Sunday finest—clean blue jeans and their best flannel shirts.

"Good morning, Preacher," shouted the congregation.

"Good morning, sinners," he replied.

He walked down the aisle, his black cowboy boots sounding solidly on the wooden floor.

He knelt in front of the burlap sacks, bowed his head, and prayed silently.

He rose, walked around the altar table, and faced the congregation. A white-laced linen cloth covered the tabernacle. On the middle of the table was a black leather-bound Bible. On one end of the table was a wood carving of hands folded in prayer; on the other, a cross of twisted barbed wire. He opened the Bible and read: "Mark, Chapter sixteen, Verses seventeen to eighteen, 'And these signs will follow who believe. In my name they will drive out demons; they will speak in new tongues; they will pick up snakes with their hands and drink deadly poison and it will not hurt them at all; they will place their hands on the sick people, and they will get well.'

"This is the word of the Lord."

"Amen," shouted the congregation.

"Hands, hands, hands," Preacher Jacob addressed the congregation. "The word is used twice. Pick up serpents with your hands. Place their hands on the sick and heal. And what do we have here on this white linen?" He picked up the sculpture and extended it toward the congregation. "Hands praying. Carved out of the pines God made."

He set the hands gently on the table. "And how did He, the Almighty, create these pines? By scattering pine cones…seeds with hands."

"Amen, Preacher, Amen," shouted the congregation.

"We shake hands when we meet. We dry our tears with our hands. We make love with our hands, caressing our lover. And God said this is good." Preacher Jacob raised his hands over his head. "And we praise the Lord with our hands."

The congregation stood up, raised their hands, and burst out chanting, "Preacher Jacob, Preacher Jacob, Preacher Jacob." They stomped on the wooden floor. The altar table and the entire room rattled.

Preacher Jacob slowly lowered his hands and waited for the frenzy to subside. The congregation sat down. He waited until the only sound was the background rattle from the burlap sacks. He spoke softly. "How will demons be driven out? By the laying on of hands."

He looked up at the overhead lamps and then down at the burlap sacks. "And what do you smell here? The odor of kerosene or the stench of the vermin imprisoned in these sacks?"

Dean stood up and said, "The lord of the flies, Preacher Jacob."

"Amen," answered the congregation.

"Yes," continued Preacher Jacob. "The lord of the flies. The lord of vermin. She. Yes she, the devil. Her stench will snuff out the sweetest fragrance. She will overpower our nostrils and us poor sinners."

Pointing his finger and reaching over to the barbed wire cross, he pricked the tip. Then raised his finger over the table. A drop of blood oozed out and splattered onto the white linen. "This cross. This cross is our salvation."

"Praise the Lord!"

"Now is the time to test our faith against these demons." Preacher Jacob walked around the table and knelt to untie the ropes that secured the three burlap sacks.

The serpents slithered out onto the wooden floor.

Chapter 9

Josh pulled off the two-lane highway at the intersection of M-72 and Little Dipper Road, attracted by another roadkill. He opened the pickup door, stepped onto the gravel shoulder, and walked down to the bird lying on the grass. A red-tailed hawk with a squirrel impaled in its black talons, the hunter and victim both dead. Probably from the perch of a telephone pole, she had been preying upon the abundant game scurrying across the blacktop.

He knelt beside her. A female, he guessed, because of her size, raptor females being a third larger than males. He picked her up by one wing, grabbed the other wing, and spread them apart, easily a four-foot span. With the squirrel clamped in her claws, he held her high above his head, her final soaring display for the passing cars, drivers slowing down to a crawl either waving, giving a thumbs-up, or honking while he carried her to his pickup to lay her in the bed. One wing was bruised; the other, not a vein ruffled, and the tail feathers, perfect. Joyce would be ecstatic. She used the wing feathers of red-tails in her blessing ceremonies.

The clock in his cab read 12:15. He'd be a few minutes late for his lunch date with Joyce at the Peace Gathering.

The Peace Gathering was a one-story green cinder block sprawling over several acres next to a small lake, Little Dipper Lake, about the size of a football field. The only wired enclosure was a fenced-in cage that secured police when processing a new admission.

He parked in the visitor parking space, walked over to the entrance, opened the door to the outer foyer, and pressed the buzzer. The receptionist asked who it was and buzzed the door open. He had visited Joyce here for lunch several times.

"Cell phone please," the receptionist said.

Josh handed over his cell phone.

He was surprised how casually everyone was dressed, including the detainees—blue jeans and sweatshirts. He despised the term "prisoner." And he was amazed how well behaved the boys were. Most were from unhappy and violent families, and when taken out of that caldron called a home and treated with kindness, they changed. It was only after they were released and had to return to their homes that the vicious cycle of violence could erupt again.

He entered the cafeteria, which was surrounded by a plate glass window, allowing a view of Little Dipper Lake encircled by a dense stand of white pine.

Josh picked up a tray, served himself through the cafeteria line, walked over to the table, and sat down next to Joyce.

"You're late," she said.

"I picked up a roadkill. A red-tailed hawk not too far from here. I laid her in the back of my pickup. Some nice wing and tail feathers intact."

"Oh, thank you, thank you, thank you. But how odd," she said. "I was just reading a poem by one of my students, John Littleton, a very sensitive boy, to Chuck here."

Josh nodded and Chuck nodded back. Chuck Mansfield had been the warden ever since he'd met Joyce. He held that quiet Native American reserve Josh had come to know and, yes, respect. In that simple gesture he'd said, "We know each other. No hand shaking or talking is necessary. We are friends."

"I'll start reading again from the beginning."

RAPTURE RIVER

Blood River Hawk

Tail of Redness
Deep Blood Red
Perch, Prey, Pierce
In Cold Blood
Till the Sacrifice
Pale of Life
Delivered by
The Dark White Angel
The Redness Splashing
From the High Holy Table
Into the Blood Red Swamp
Foaming into the Madness
Of Red Death

Joyce paused and looked out the window at the lake. "He's only fifteen years old. He was raised by his mother, a Muslim… There I go. No matter what she is. She did a fine job of raising him, the best she could. His father, Native American, Ojibwa, committed suicide with a shotgun when John was eight years old. John found him on the back porch of their home a bloody mess."

"Terribly sad," Josh said. "How long has he been here?"

"Three months."

"For what?"

"Drunk and disorderly. He ran away into Van Horn's swamp. Hid out for a week. Jed Lewis found him and helped Sheriff Mad bring him in."

"Jedidiah Lewis," Josh said. "I'm learning more daily about this holy man."

"Lewis is fine if he's not drinking," Joyce said. "He has an uncanny rapport with the boys. They never get violent with Lewis.

I...I don't know how he does it."

Chuck extended his hand toward Josh and said, "Yesterday...a boy kicked out all the back seat windows of a patrol car. If Lewis was there, that wouldn't happen."

Joyce stood up. "Not to kill any more time, but my one o'clock class starts in five minutes. We'll be talking about this poem. Maybe you'd like to sit in and observe. If that's okay with Chuck."

Chuck nodded.

The classroom reminded Josh of his grade school, St. Thomas—eight round tables seating six at each. All boys between the ages of thirteen and nineteen. Most, from what he could guess, were Native American. A plate glass window extended the length of the outside wall that looked out upon a dense stand of white pine. Josh sat in the back of the class next to the window. Joyce stood off to the side of the front wall, upon which was mounted a TV screen and a white board, not chalk and blackboard, but felt pens and plastic.

John Littleton walked to the front of the class and read his poem. After saying the last word, "death," he looked at Joyce and then at Josh.

"Thank you, John," Joyce said.

John sat down.

She looked over the class. "Any comments."

"Very violent," one of the boys said.

"Violence. That's why we're here. That's why I'm here," Joyce said. "I'm here by my own choice. But you're not. So let's talk about violence. Is the red-tailed hawk to be hated because he is violent? Or is he misunderstood as maybe we are?"

"It depends upon what he feeds on," John said. "If he's feeding on a snake, we...at least I...cheer him on. I hate snakes. But if he's after a mourning dove, I hope the dove gets away."

"Thank you, John," Joyce said. She walked over to the window and looked up at the white pines. "We admire them in flight, their soaring, their freedom, but we have difficulty accepting their violence. They look fierce with their hooked beaks and sharp talons. We say they look mean. But nature is not a tame little puppy. It is a violent world. And we even call it cruel. It is natural for them to hunt…and for us to hunt. Hawks have been given a bum rap, but I see beauty in their cold-blooded, savage violence.

"Does that scare you? I've studied words and what they mean for years. My master's degree in linguistics taught me that not every feeling we have can be expressed in words. Sometimes all we have are our gut-level animal instincts.

"We name our football teams after them—The Falcons, The Seahawks, The Panthers, The Eagles, The Lions, The Wolfpack. We identify with their cunning, strength, and beauty but not their violence. Violence is a part of nature. It is nature. We put our violence off to the side because we don't want to see it. That chicken we had for lunch got there on our plates because of the violence to the chicken. We allow someone else to do our violence for us, kill the chicken…or maybe a machine that we created."

Josh raised his hand. "Can I participate?"

"Yes. Sure, Josh."

"In a recent movie I saw, in the credits at the end, the comment was made that no harm or violence was inflicted upon the animals, even the fish, in the movie. And yet we view violence daily on TV—burning inner cities, rioting, suicide bombings, humans jumping off a building. Are we the dumb animals, bird brains? And yet we view the hawk or osprey as violent."

"That's a good point," Joyce said. "And that brings us to the question: Who am I? What is my nature? There was an author, Jonathan Swift, who lived 275 years ago in Ireland. He wrote a novel, *Gulliver's Travels*. In the first part Gulliver travels to a land of dwarfs, and he is a giant. In the second part he travels to a land of giants, and Gulliver is a dwarf. He looks at the world from two viewpoints, and he sees the world as two utterly dissimilar places.

"We are looking at the world from the inside of a prison. Those on the outside look at us, inside. We have two opposites here. How do we view them? How do they view us?

"There's another book written by William Golding in 1954. About two hundred years after *Gulliver's Travels*, *The Lord of the Flies*. In that book we also look at our human nature. A group of boys are stranded on an island and revert to the violence that has been kept in check by society. Are we a violent species? The hawk doesn't think about his nature. He's a hunter, a bird of prey. His violent nature is determined by us. We call him violent. But are we basically the same way? Is our violence kept in check only by laws, the police, and the society in which we live?"

Chuck opened the door, entered the room, closed the door slowly behind him, and leaned against it.

Joyce continued. "I don't know if we will ever solve this problem. All we may do is ask more questions. Are we more violent than not violent? Are we more evil than good? There I go again. Am I saying that evil is violence? I'm crossed in my own arguments. These are all questions that man has been struggling with for a long time. Just what is our nature? Our human nature.

"This is serious business. And now let's take a break from all this thinking. Let's continue with our movie, *The Lord of the Rings*." The class clapped.

Chuck looked at Josh and nodded. He opened the door, walked into the hall. He waved at Josh.

Josh followed him out of the room and closed the door.

They stood face-to-face in the empty hallway.

"There's been another murder," Chuck said. "His throat was slit."

"On the river?"

"Yes."

"The sheriff is looking for Ted. I told him you were here. He asked me to ask you."

"I left him fishing at Crocket Rapids this morning. I'll be picking him up later."

"He has a cell phone?"

"Ted never carries it. Leaves it at his cabin. He prefers smoke signals. More reliable. They forced one on him for his parole duties."

"Sounds like him," Chuck said.

"I'll find Ted."

Chapter 10

Josh knelt and dipped his cupped hands into the icy spring. He raised the water to his lips and drank, the coldness dripping onto his chin and wetting his red chamois shirt. He looked up at the quaking aspen, its leaves fluttering in a slight breeze. The spring itself, alongside the gravel road near Crocket Rapids Bridge, was Ted's birthday present to Josh one warm Sunday morning. After he had celebrated Mass at the mission church, Ted had taken him fishing but before wading into the stream had led him to a hidden spring that bubbled up alongside a deer trail. "I've never given this to anybody. Happy birthday. I named it after my wife, Angelica's Fountain," he remembered Ted saying. The only words Ted had said that afternoon on the river. Ted had revealed an intimate part of himself, and Josh felt that he had the father he never had or at least could remember. He never saw or even touched his father. His father died in an automobile accident on his way to the hospital as Josh was being born. Josh was his mother's first and only child.

He had parked at the bridge and walked uphill on the deer trail to the spring. A pair of crows alighted on the crown of an adjacent red maple, their caws echoing down the river. It was six o'clock. Ted would probably be wading upstream back to the bridge, fishing the early evening hatches with dry flies. Josh walked downstream along the bank to meet him.

RAPTURE RIVER

The trail along the river was deeply rutted with deer hooves. Whitetails had tracked on this path for over a hundred years. Loggers' journals from the late 1800s illustrated with detailed sketches the trails that deer and bear had used.

The path was firm and dry on the bank. At one point the trail descended until it dipped down to the river's level, where black muck sucked at his heels. The scattered prints of deer pooled water into heart-shaped puddles. Off to the side was a large scat and a double-rutted bear trail in the grass that meandered into the swamp. He stepped into a bear track. His size nine boot extended an inch beyond the print—a huge animal.

The trail rose from river to a path, a section of the North Country Pathway, which meandered around a hillside. On the peak of the hill, known as Rattlesnake Bluff, large boulders lay scattered over its baldness—sun decks for rattlers on hot summer days. He sat on one of the boulders and looked down upon the river spreads. The main branch divided into rivulets, finger-like divisions, which coursed over a grassy plain—the Michigan everglades. In the dwindling light, Ted was in the middle of a rivulet and casting upstream.

"Hey, Ted." His voice carried easily and pierced the evening calm.

He looked up and waved. "Josh."

He made his way upstream, climbed the bank, and trudged up the path that led to the peak of Rattlesnake Bluff, Molly at his side.

Josh walked down to greet him as he struggled up, breathing heavily.

Ted stopped and leaned on his walking stick. "Thanks. I needed my walking stick and a little push."

"Hey, Molly," Josh said. "Remember when we first met on the river, under that cedar? You didn't have Molly yet."

"Never forget that afternoon. I didn't have any luck then either. I guess some days we never forget, always remember. Now Molly, my faithful companion."

They sat on a boulder and looked down upon the spreads—the gold of the grasses and the silver reflection of the setting sun upon water.

"Any luck?"

"This is my luck, looking down upon this river valley. But no fish…maybe tomorrow. So, why are you out here, looking for me? I can still take care of myself… No worry there."

Josh said, "There's been another murder."

"How?"

"The victim's throat was slit."

Ted nodded. "I thought so. I saw Coop. He came up to me by the river and kept running his hand across his throat." Ted shook his head. "No one can talk to Coop. Or in some way communicate with him. He'll spook. But then there's Jedidiah Lewis. He's the only one who might get through."

Chapter 11

Josh was standing on the sidewalk outside the Pregnancy Crisis Aid Center. It was 4:45 p.m., Friday. His week had been busy but a refreshing break from the river madness of the previous week. He was waiting for the last patient and gazing out upon the Lake Michigan whitecaps of Grand Traverse Bay. A yellow kayak was bobbing on the surf. Traverse City was sixty miles from the Black River.

The Pregnancy Crisis Aid Center was in an old, renovated post office, a one-story redbrick building. The US Post Office sign that had hung over the entrance had been replaced with the logo of the center—an egg held by two hands inside of which was an infant with a full head of black hair. Scrolled above the egg was "Help" in capital letters. Below the egg were the words "Pregnancy Crisis Aid." "Crisis" and "help" had a negative connotation, as if a catastrophe had fallen upon someone. Josh hoped to change those words but had only been employed here one year. Women Now, the abortion clinic two blocks down the street, drew more clients simply because their sign had more appeal. The girls who mistakenly entered that clinic were kindly referred to Josh. They were both in the business of babies, but Josh's Aid Center was a free service supported by local churches and charities. Women Now was business for profit.

He reentered the building. The receptionist, Jan, was on the phone.

He walked back to his office to wait for his last appointment. His room, without any windows, was furnished in, what he called, Early Goodwill. He sat down on a wobbly swivel chair behind his oak desk, marred with deep gouges. How did those groves get there? Who and what and with what? A dull blade. On the wall opposite his desk was a painting of Jesus smiling. There were days when he saw Jesus smiling, and other days when he was laughing. Laughing at what? Jan buzzed his room to inform him that his last patient had arrived. He told her to send her back. His door was open.

She entered the open doorway and set her patient folder on his desk. She was noticeably pregnant, the last trimester. But her wrap-around sunglasses, beaded headband with a partridge tail fanned above her left ear, and a wing of a red-tailed hawk secured above her right ear did not mask her identity. She slid the office chair next to the table and perched on the edge. That close, he picked up on her aroma, a combination of jade, sweetgrass, and lavender—wild and sensual. And he knew it was Joyce, her pregnancy enhanced with a pillow. He'd counsel her. He had to.

He shuffled through the papers in her health history and looked up at her. "And so…"

"And so…it's spring. The red-tailed hawks have nested with their mates, as have I." She looked at the painting on the wall of Jesus laughing. "Why is he laughing?"

"I've always wondered about that. If he's smiling or laughing at something." He rubbed a deep gouge in the table. "If he's laughing, maybe he's laughing at the folly of humanity, at his own humanness."

"Then, were we created as a joke?"

"We were created in his own image."

"Let's see now. Follow the order of creation. He created the monkeys and was entertained by their antics, but he thought he could do better. He kept some of their basic physiology but added more gray matter, and along came us, and we were hilarious. What a show. He had a perfect comedy." She paused and smiled. "Didn't this portrait of Jesus first appear in *Playboy*? And were you reading *Playboy* when you first saw it?"

"It could have appeared in *Playboy.*"

"Well, maybe you picked up and skimmed through it."

"Maybe. But let's talk about why you're here."

"I'm here because my lover is headless."

"Headless!"

"Not the head of his… That's more than adequate. There are times I wanted to tell him that he was more than adequate. But telling him would probably cause his insecurities to rise. You see at one time he was a Catholic priest."

"Shouldn't we be talking more about you and the child?"

"No!"

"Why?"

"Because part of him is inside me. He and I created this egg. And I need him to help build my nest."

"So what species of bird are you?"

"Are you trying to evade the subject again? What difference does it make? If I had my way, I'd be a red-tailed hawk."

"Why?"

"Because of their mating rituals. But I'd have the parenting instincts of a partridge. The female is evasive with her broken wing act. She draws a potential enemy to herself to give her young a chance to escape. She sacrifices herself."

"All birds have mating rituals."

"But hawks are unique. They soar high up together, and at the moment they reach their peak, they interlock their talons and hold onto each other and then free fall to the earth. I'm sure it's the female who initiates the maneuver and the letting go, just before crashing onto the ground. You better have some excitement. Having babies isn't easy. Not just some momentary sex, even though that's fun too."

"The male must have some role in initiating this maneuver."

"If he knows how to deal...and he knows. He'll bring her a dead mourning dove. And her thanks is their soaring and coupling... Doesn't that just take your breath away?"

"Where is all this bird talk getting us to?"

Joyce stood up and walked over to the picture of Jesus laughing. She looked at Josh and took off her glasses.

"I knew it was you," he said.

"I knew you knew."

"I didn't go to Women Now down the street. Unless you want me to?"

"No. You came to the right place."

"Then counsel me."

His chair teetered as he leaned back. "Marry me."

"That's not counseling. That's a command. You have to show me the way, as Hiawatha showed us the way."

"Hiawatha?"

"There's no monopoly on your Christ. There have been many way-showers. Hiawatha had an earthly mother and the Great Spirit for a Father. Who besides Christ has shown you the way?"

"The yogis and yoga have been my guides."

"Well, tell me."

"When I was in the seminary, my roommate gave me a book, *Christian Yoga.*"

"Not Native American Yoga."

"Well, I thought of that. Is yoga profane? For heathens. Why do we define the world from only one perspective—ours or yours? Why not, let's say, from the perspective of the pygmy?"

RAPTURE RIVER

"Pygmy!"

"Does that bother you, Joyce? Or are the African pygmies so far different from you that you may even be prejudiced. God forbid."

"You're trying to avoid the subject."

"Which is Christian yoga—"

"No," she said. "Is that why I saw you standing on your head? I thought it was to calm your heathen desires when I wasn't immediately available."

"Maybe it does. But let's get back to the perspective of *Christian Yoga*. The book was written by a French Benedictine monk. The book has the Church's approval, in France—the nihil obstat, nothing objectionable. But the French are liberal."

"And ingenious. They perfected perfume. And claim to have invented negligee. When I was…yes, attired…with only feathers, my Native American version of lace was appealing to you. Wasn't the black and red contrast exciting? Your head is beginning to turn red. Your head."

"Joyce!"

"*Bkaagiid.*"

"What does that mean?"

"Ask my grandmother."

"I will."

"And oh! French kissing. You enjoyed that so much. I had to teach you!"

"Wasn't I a good student?"

"You were an excellent student. And very innovative, exploring other spaces with your tongue. Native Americans have one Great Spirit, who is in everything. We don't have a book to guide us. Consequently, we don't argue about God. We are part animal. We are mammals. We are part of that creation. And we respect the spirit. We don't adore a rock, but the spirit behind the rock."

His phone rang and Jan said, "It's 5:30. I'm going home. I'll lock up. How's it going with your patient?"

"Fine," he said. "Go ahead. And I'll take the lights off. We'll be finished in a few minutes."

They sat in silence and heard Jan start her car.

Joyce unwrapped herself and placed her blanket on the arm of the chair. She stood up and removed the pillow and placed it on the floor. She pushed her chair off to the side, took her blanket, and spread it below the pillow. "We're alone."

"Yes, we are."

"Our nesting place. We're ground birds. Like Kirkland warblers, penned into this little room. Now close your eyes. Don't open them until I say so."

He closed his eyes.

After a few minutes she said, "Now open your eyes."

He opened his eyes.

She stood in front of him clad only in a red tail dangling by a leather thong below her navel.

He rose from the chair.

Chapter 12

On Saturday morning Josh drove to Peshawbestown to see Joyce at her grandmother's. He had only visited her twice over the past year. The fog was thick and M-22, Bay Shore Drive, the two-lane blacktop that meandered along the Lake Michigan shore of the Leelanau peninsula, was lonely.

The peninsula, on the northern border of Traverse City, was thirty miles long and averaged about seven miles across. Bay Shore Drive stretched along the eastern side of the peninsula. The land had a favorable climate for growing cherries and yearly harvested the world's largest tart cherry crop. But that position was threatened by the appetite of land developers. Condos were sprouting up rather than cherry trees. Shacks along the lakeshore were being bought at a premium dollar for the property only, and million-dollar summer homes were under construction. Golf courses were rolling out over the farmland.

Midway up the peninsula lay the village of Suttons Bay with its marina. It spoke prosperity. Small shops, like Bay Wear, promised that your image would blend in with sailing.

Ten miles north was Peshawbestown. The sign simply read—Peshawbestown. No population numbers given. A general store within a gas station, a natural resource fish station, and the Michigan Sands Casino, a solid brick structure with a gabled roof on a hillside, overlooked the reservation. Most of the traffic stopped here at the casino. Those who passed were on their way to either the next marina at Northport Village or to Lighthouse Point at the tip of the peninsula and Leelanau State Park.

All this belied the essence of the peninsula—Peshawbestown, anxiously hidden amongst this opulence. Behind the casino, hidden in the hills, a subdivision was plotted, and one-story, modest frame homes were being built. Corner street signs like Ojibway Way and Eagle Lane were posted at every intersection. The development was centered around a dome-shaped pavilion—The Meeting Place. At the entrance to the village was a redbrick health facility—the Medicine Lodge. All compliments of the casino.

Joyce's grandmother didn't live there. She lived down from the casino along the Lake Michigan shoreline in a modest trailer home that Joyce had bought for her.

Josh turned right from Bay Shore Drive onto the gravel driveway. Joyce's red Prius was off to the side. Her gambling talents at the casino had provided her with financial security. He parked next to her Prius. It was 9:00 a.m. He opened the door, stepped down on the gravel, walked over to the wood steps, climbed the steps, and knocked.

Joyce's ninety-eight-year-old grandmother promptly opened the door. "Shh…she's sleeping," she said. "Joyce got in early this morning. She worked at the casino. A long poker game with some high rollers from Detroit and Chicago. She took them."

He walked in and closed the door. She led him to a table. "Sit down. I'll get us a cup of coffee."

He sat down. Three pine chairs set around a circular slab sawed from a pine stump with a twisted labyrinth of roots that served as its legs, the table in front of a large bay window, on the center a totemic wooden bird.

She walked over with a tray of coffee and some type of roll, set it on the table, and sat down. Her face was deeply lined, but she was agile. Her fingernails neatly manicured. "You like my new manicure?" She flashed her nails in front of Josh. "Joyce took me over to the new Chinese manicure parlor in Traverse. Did you know that the Chinese first used nail polish? I asked for the same shade of red as Joyce's car." She picked up her cup of coffee, took a sip, and looked out the window.

"Shanaya, you haven't changed," Josh said. "It's been a year since I saw you last."

"The thunderbirds returned again this spring." She picked up the totemic figure. "Joyce bought this for me in Alaska last winter when she was researching Native American languages. We may not speak exactly the same but we have the same mythology." She handed the figure to Josh. "It's carved out of old-growth yellow Alaskan cedar. Their spirits live with the sun above. They give rain and lightning and thunder. They create and destroy. They fly to warm climates in winter and return in spring, to give life."

The figure was about six inches long. The wings were folded along its side. A large black beak protruded between two black eyes. On the back was a lid.

"Open the lid," she said. "A totemic box."

He opened the lid. "Such fine craftsmanship."

"Gifts are found in the box. Joyce, of course."

He removed a rolled-up bill and handed it to her.

She unraveled it. "A hundred-dollar bill. Joyce did very well. A tip last night."

She placed the bill under the totem and looked out the window. "She's struggling this morning. *Giizis*, the sun. Working her way up over the tree line across the bay. Much fog to burn off this morning, a big job ahead, a sacred job."

"Joyce should be working her way up soon."

"She'll sleep for a while after a long night at the casino. I raised

Joyce. Her mother, my last child, died when she was born. So I was her mother. My husband, her grandfather, died when she was sixteen.

"I was a lot like Joyce when I was her age. Of course, there weren't the opportunities then as now. I had thirteen children. Two of them were stillborn. But I love them the same. They are alive within me."

"You know, of course, her spirit guide."

"A hawk. A red-tailed hawk."

"Yes. She loved their fierceness, gentleness, and playfulness. She was in New York last year at Columbia University doing research. She told me about the New Yorkers' fascination with a pair of redtails that nested in the city. They built their nest on the window ledge of an exclusive apartment on Fifth Avenue. That confirmed her spirit guide. They were as adaptable as she was. They had no boundaries."

Joyce opened her bedroom door and walked down the hall to the table. Her pet skunk, Lady Slipper, followed her.

Her grandmother poured her coffee.

Joyce sat down. Lady Slipper slid under the table and clawed into a tangle of roots. "Her favorite resting place. A little hammock of roots." She looked out the window. "You can barely see the trees across the bay through the fog. The roots remain the same, only the leaves change. And we're rooted. Aren't we, Lady Slipper?"

"You did well last night." Josh tapped the $100 bill on the table.

"A tip from the chief executive at Garfield Energy. He drank and talked. Drank bloody Marys and talked some more. One of the guards had to escort him to his hotel room. No, almost carry him."

Lady Slipper squealed. Josh looked under the table. "Hey there, girl. Good to see you again. I never said it but aren't they illegal as pets in Michigan?"

"Illegal for whom?"

"For somebody else, of course."

Joyce patted her with her foot, and she responded by wrapping her paw around Joyce's big toe. "Lady Slipper was the sole survivor of a road-killed litter, just down the road. Lewis helped me nurse it. He has an uncanny manner with all creatures."

"I love caring for her," Shanaya said. "She's a little stinker. Play hide and seek with you when it's time for her bath. But she's fun."

"Not to change the subject." Josh looked at Joyce's grandmother. "What does '*bkaagiid*' mean?"

She smiled. "Should I tell him, Joyce?"

Joyce hesitated, turned slowly toward Josh, and nodded.

"It means...it means too much sex."

Joyce looked under the table at Lady Slipper. "The big stink now is about ruining the river with oil and the other murder. Nature is self-cleansing but sometimes with our help, as with Lady Slipper."

Josh was tempted to ask how she felt, but that would only bring up the issue of her pregnancy. Should he ask for her grandmother's blessing? But that would come in time without asking. So as Joyce appeared to be entering one of her trances, he interrupted and asked, "Did the executive from Garfield Energy say anything about the murders?"

She looked at Josh, lifted her coffee cup and drank. "He was so drunk. He rambled on and on about the murders. Both murders were on federal land. That's a plus for Garfield Energy. They would rather work with the federal people than the local sheriff. They have already found out that there's a clairvoyant in the area who had worked with a federal marshal. A psychic who had assisted with a rape case down south. He's up here visiting his daughter and setting up a mission church—a religious sect of serpent handlers."

"That would be the Signs Followers," Josh said. "We may not understand their religion, but it is biblically based. They have a very deep faith."

"Well," Joyce said, "I prefer turtles over rattlesnakes."

Chapter 13

Federal Marshal John McClelan stopped his SUV on the summit of the hill above the mission church. He turned off the engine, opened the door, stepped onto the grass, and looked down upon the valley. A lone car was parked off to the side. It was 4:00 p.m. and the Sunday congregation had dispersed. A tall black figure casting an equally long shadow appeared from behind the church. McClelan knew it was Reverend Jacob. He had always enjoyed talking with the reverend because they were the same height, six feet four, no looking down, just eye to eye.

He had flown into Traverse City the week before and at his first meeting with Garfield Energy had met Sheriff Mad. The sheriff's casual remark that there was a Reverend Jacob starting up a mission church of snake handlers and that they should be investigated had led him here on this lonely Sunday afternoon. He had worked with Reverend Jacob and, with the reverend's psychic powers, had solved a rape-murder case in North Carolina.

He reentered his vehicle, drove down the hill, and parked alongside Reverend Jacob's car. He remained behind the wheel as Reverend Jacob walked over.

"John McClelan. So good to see you again. Get out of that car, kneel on the grass, and I'll give you my blessing."

"Reverend Jacob." John knelt down on the grass.

The reverend placed both hands on his temples. "May the spirit shield you from the vermin of the earth. May the Archangel Gabriel lay upon you the blessings of his sword so that you may walk in the radiance of his light and no harm will come to you." He pressed on his temples and then released. "Now rise and stand."

He stood up and they embraced, hugging each other in silence.

Finally, the reverend said, "How did you find me? And why are you here in the first place? Let's go over to the church steps and talk."

They walked over to the steps and sat down. The sun illuminated the steps and doorway to the church, shrouding them in a phosphorescent radiance.

"That sun is bright," John said. "And to bring a little more sun into your life, I have a little something for you. When I found out you were here, I called the boys back in Washington and told them about your mission church here. We took up a collection; here's a check for $976, an offering."

"Why, thank you kindly," said the reverend, placing the check in his shirt pocket. "And…"

"And what brings me here? I was assigned the murders here that were committed on federal land. I found out you were here, so here I am. And you can probably guess why."

"You want my help again."

"Yes."

"To help solve these murders."

"Yes." John looked at the burlap sacks stacked against the church.

The reverend smiled. "Don't worry, John. They're tied tightly. I am a man of many faiths and tolerate all faiths. But I have found the deepest faith I have seen is the faith of the Signs Followers. Someday you may convert."

"I'm not ready…yet. Probably never."

The reverend smiled. "Nevertheless. Yes, I will help you."

"Thank you."

"How far is the murder site from here?"

"A couple of miles."

"Let's go there now. Spontaneity is important. No analyzing. No guessing. Pure psychic energy. We'll get there before sundown. Twilight. We may even stay there until the witching hour. And it's near a full moon. Perfect timing. Let's go."

They drove down the two-track to the most recent murder site. The shadows of white pines slanted across the trail, enshrouding them in a black pall.

John stopped at a clearing. "This is it."

They sat in silence.

A yellow Caterpillar tractor was off to the side.

Finally, the reverend opened the door, stepped down on the grass, and carefully closed the door. He whispered, "Sit there while I look around."

He walked over to the tractor, circled it, and then sat down on the front bumper. He remained motionless until the sun set. He knelt down and crawled over to the far end of the clearing. He stood up on the high bank overlooking the river. A full moon illuminated the river below. He looked out into the distance at the sparkling, tortuous route—a dark highway lighted through the swamp. He stood there staring into the distance. Then a numbing sensation in his forehead along with the mantra sic-um, sic-um rattled inside his head, and he was brought down to his knees. He continued to stare into

RAPTURE RIVER

the swamp, but no image appeared—only the labyrinthine glow of the river flamed before him.

He rose slowly from his knees and walked back to the car, waved at John to come out, and sat down on the bumper of the tractor.

John sat next to him.

"Nothing," said the reverend.

"Nothing?"

"The rain had washed away any trace. We didn't get here soon enough. And nothing was left behind."

"They found nothing," John said.

"Let's sit here till midnight," the reverend said.

Chapter 14

Josh parked his pickup on the fringe of the casino parking lot. Sunday morning and this was his sanctuary for worship—a gambling casino.

He looked at his rearview mirror and adjusted his black hairpiece, pressed his beard firmly into place, tightening the elastic slider that secured it. Would she see through his disguise as he saw through hers? She was in the poker room until 4:00 a.m., off four hours, and then back again at the blackjack table at eight. A little sleep deprivation could help. He had dwelled upon the last detail of his disguise, camouflaging his hands with self-tanning lotion. His throaty voice of a middle-aged logger was his most difficult ploy. Attired in a flannel shirt and blue jean work pants with red suspenders, he tromped up to the entrance in his hiking boots. Gait was as important as appearance. And he swung the door open.

"Good morning, sir. Welcome. Nice seeing you again," the doorman said.

"You remember."

"We always remember our best customers," the doorman replied.

Josh had snuck in on Joyce's day off to learn the rudiments of blackjack. He'd decided against poker, too emotionally involved and too snarly for his taste, like untying a knotted leader. Blackjack was the most popular non-slot machine game in the house. He'd downloaded rules of blackjack and read them over and sat down at a table one morning to test his disguise and pick up what he could on the game. Everyone at that table was willing to teach the neophyte, which he openly admitted he was. What better way to learn. The dealer at first went over the rudiments of the game and even got into some sophisticated maneuvers as insurance which he didn't understand. It was about to bet whether the dealer has twenty-one right off the bat. But he'd get by without that. Keep it simple. Besides, maybe best if he did seem a little dense about the game. The gambler he'd sat next to was intense. Once her hand was dealt, a deep-seated daemon grasped her soul, and her focal point was her cards—a bear guarding her cubs.

Josh stood in the elevated foyer on the carpet patterned with maple leaves. The grand gambling room was decorated to create a wilderness atmosphere. Stained glass windows above were etched with clumps of cedar and birch trees. On the far rock wall was a waterfall splashing down onto a rivulet which flowed around an island of reclining chairs with a log bridge for access.

Slot machines took in most of the revenue, but they lacked the human element of surprise and ambush, and, at times, on the blackjack tables, the emotions ran high. The blackjack tables, six kidney-shaped tables with seven stools, were in the middle of the casino surrounded by the slot machines. The dealers stood in the oval of the kidney. Joyce was at the end table on his right surrounded by five gamblers. She looked very becoming in her blue casino shirt, her black braid tied into a bun on her head, and her dangling gold earrings. She was dwarfed by some very hefty gamblers, but her presence dominated. She had put on the aura of the blackjack shark. He decided not to play at her table initially. He'd case the joint out and slowly sink into the atmosphere.

He wandered over to the end table at the opposite end from Joyce and stood there next to a tall, bald man dressed in his Sunday finest—white shirt, black tie, navy blazer, black pants.

"Did you just come from early Sunday services?" Josh asked.

"No," he answered. "This is my church. Zeke here."

"Samson."

"Samson?"

"Yes, Samson."

"Did your mother give you that name because you were born with a full head of hair? I'm envious."

"I always wondered about that. And Zeke, from the biblical Ezekial?"

"In answer to your question about church. This is my religion now. I am summoned by all these bells ringing, lights flashing. My church bells now and my candles. Real church bells are a thing of my past," Zeke said.

"I am surprised at the number of people in church, I mean the casino, on this early Sunday morning."

"I'm not," Zeke said. "I'll tell you with a story, a true story. In a small town in Kansas, a tornado blasted through, and on one street there was a bar and just down the road a church. Guess what the tornado took down. Of course, the church. So nobody could go to that church, and a small group of the congregation met at the bar. And they talked and asked why the church and not the bar. And some said that the evil in the bar was more apparent and visible like drunkenness and fights and maybe picking up someone. Whereas the evil in the church was a more subtle evil as slander or snubbing someone—a more vicious and hurtful evil."

Josh nodded. "There's some truth to that."

"You know what I was once?"

"What?"

"A minister at a church in South Carolina. A Baptist minister. I was thrown out of the church. Expelled."

"Why?"

"I'm bipolar. I have bipolar disorder. Manic depression. Then I didn't know it. After the diagnosis I'm more stable on lithium. I would get up in the middle of a sermon and lead my congregation down the street, even in the rain, praising the Lord. Now I don't even go to church. Bells ringing, lights flashing, coins clinking—all have a soothing effect on my mood disorder. I don't enter here with an edge. My paranoia is in check. I'm okay, you're okay.

"Well, let's get into some action," Zeke said.

Josh glanced at the other side and saw two empty seats at Joyce's table. "Over there. I'm just a rookie, so I may need some help at blackjack."

Zeke nodded.

They walked over to the table, pulled up the stools, and sat down.

"Gentlemen, what will it be," Joyce said.

Josh handed her a twenty-dollar bill. "Four five-dollar tokens," he grumbled.

She smiled. "Sir, you must place the bill on the table. For the overhead cameras."

Josh laid it down. And wondered with that smile if she knew.

She picked up the twenty and turned it over twice and placed it President Jackson side face up. "For the cameras." She smiled.

Was she playing with him? She bowed when he'd lost that trout.

"Cash in," she shouted.

A tall Native American young man walked over to Joyce's table and picked up the twenty. Joyce laid down four five-dollar tokens.

Zeke had laid down six one-hundred-dollar bills that Joyce had handled in the same manner as Josh's.

"Twelve fifty-dollar tokens," he said.

There were no smiles with Zeke. Maybe she knew already. But maybe Zeke had gambled at her table before.

They were ready to play. On the table in front of each player was an oval inscribed with either an eagle, bear, turtle, deer, rabbit, or wolf. She hit the table in front of each of the players. Josh slid one token on the eagle oval in front of him.

"Sir, you must take your fingers off your bets after you place them."

Josh drew his hand back. She knew he was a rookie. But did she know?

She withdrew the cards from the shoe, placed one down and one up on the empty oval in front of her. And then dealt each of the players two cards face up. Zeke had placed four fifty-dollar tokens on the table.

The cards lay on the table on each gambler's oval. Joyce hesitated then looked at the gambler on her immediate right, who had a ten and three. Thirteen. She tapped the table to be hit with another card. A face card. Twenty-three. Over.

Joyce had a nine of spades face up. Josh had only to beat her.

He had an eight and three. Eleven. He tapped the table to be hit. A nine. Twenty. He passed his hand above his cards to stay.

Zeke next to Josh had a ten and two. Twelve. He tapped the table to be hit again. A seven. Nineteen. He passed.

Everyone was still in it but the first player by the time Joyce played her hand. She turned over her face-down card. A three. Twelve. And hit herself again. A ten, twenty-three. Two over twenty-one. She distributed the tokens. Placed four fifty-dollar tokens next to Zeke's tokens and one five-dollar token next to Josh's.

Josh smiled. She looked at him and smiled. He was tempted to hit the table with his fist. *Is she intimidating me?*

Another dealer walked up to the table. And Joyce was relieved. Her break time.

Josh looked at Zeke. "I have to ask you a question. Can we break?"

"Sure."

The substitute dealer placed two black tokens on each of their betting circles to reserve their places.

"A short break," Josh said.

The dealer nodded.

They stood up and walked over to the bar for a cup of coffee. Joyce entered the employee-only lounge at the far end of the casino.

"Let's talk," Josh said.

"Sure."

"Over here." He walked over to the side of the slot machine aisle. They wouldn't be overheard with all this clanking and ringing. "I have to confess something," Josh said.

"Confession is good for the soul. I've listened before. What is it?"

"I'm not me. I'm somebody else."

"How? Explain."

So he told him about his disguise and relationship with Joyce and her disguise and that he was a priest and left the priesthood. But didn't tell him the nightmare.

Zeke placed his hand on Josh's shoulder. "I'm flattered that you would confide in me. Your disguise is perfect. I would never have guessed. And your story is amazing."

"I'm actually bald. I shave my head."

"Beautiful." He laughed. "Where did you meet?"

Josh told him how they had met in church at St. Peter the Fisherman.

"I've never heard of that church. It's beautiful. We identify ourselves by what we do and not what we are. He was a disciple of Christ foremost to us, but he was a fisherman first, and fisherman of men."

"And Ezekial was a prophet in exile. As you are, Zeke."

"I am haunted by visions and may always be. But prophets in the Bible were probably bipolar. My therapy sessions were instrumental in warning me about the validity of my visions. I may always have them. I sort out the real from the unreal. And I've been lucky." He set down his coffee on the bar. "I can't drink too much of this. Too much caffeine will precipitate an episode."

How much should Josh confide in this stranger. "Let's go back to the table before Joyce gets back." Maybe it was the insecurity of a Sunday morning in a gambling casino that enticed Josh into his revelations.

They returned to the blackjack game. Their places had been saved, but another gambler had joined. Sitting next to Josh was a man with an oxygen cart behind his chair. His wife, Josh presumed, stood next to him and held a nasal inhaler. She placed it over his head, and he adjusted the tubing in each nostril.

"Any luck?" Josh asked.

"Lucky to be alive," he said. "They tell me that I only have a few months left. Maybe I should be in church, but I'm going where I'm going, and no praying will change my future."

They played two hands and then Joyce returned to deal.

After all the seven players had placed their bets, Zeke rose from his chair and raised his arms above his head. "Let them be anathema. And all you sinners repent," he shouted over the ringing bells and flashing lights.

Joyce moved back from the table.

Zeke pointed at Josh. "You are an impostor, the devil himself." He grabbed his wig and flung it on the floor and plucked off his beard and slapped it on the table. Then he swiped the table clean with his arms and scattered the chips and cards on the floor, chairs, and laps of the gamblers.

The man on oxygen next to Josh tipped his stool and tumbled onto the carpet. He landed on all fours. His wife quickly knelt, adjusted his nasal inhaler, and began picking up fifty-dollar tokens and stuffing them into his mouth. He obeyed her, obediently, like a dog, never barking, not even wagging a tail.

Three uniformed guards immediately surrounded Zeke. He continued, "This temple of vice and iniquity will be destroyed by fire and brimstone."

Two more uniformed guards surrounded Zeke. "Sir, would you please come with us," one of the guards pleaded.

Zeke pointed a finger at Josh. "Begone, Satan. I will fly with my blue angels, and my chariots will return with hellfire and brimstone." He willingly followed the guards out of the casino.

Josh picked up his beard off the table and hairpiece off the floor. Joyce smiled at him and said, "Exciting. Not dull in here. I'll be relieved after all this. I'll be at my grandmother's. Nice disguise. You paid me back. I didn't know."

"Then I'll see you shortly." And why did he ever disguise? It proved nothing. Or maybe it made both of them aware of their folly. They escaped the trap that ensnared them. And maybe this awkward childish play would stop and, yes, both would grow up.

A uniformed guard walked up to Josh and said, "The management would like to ask you a few questions, sir."

He followed him.

Josh answered their questions about the disguise and told of his relationship with Joyce. They were dismissive about his involvement with Zeke, but they took his name and address. Zeke had been under surveillance for some time as a suspicious character. They wished him luck with gambling but added that possibly it would be best to return as himself.

Chapter 15

Seagulls were gliding on the light breezes off Lake Michigan. They were walking along the shoreline of her grandmother's mobile home. Monday, Memorial Day—a day for remembering and forgetting. The sun was inching down behind the tall pines, casting long shadows on the beach.

"We may see the moon rise again," Josh said.

"Blue Moon. Moon River. The man in the moon. We face everything but each other. And we even wear masks to deceive each other. Children's play."

"I felt something after the casino masquerade."

"I did too."

"Now that makes two of us," Josh said.

"Three of us… I can't say what it was, but maybe it's a new beginning."

"Not the end."

"I would hope a new beginning. We wear masks to deceive ourselves. I had a dream again last night."

Josh stopped.

She looked up at him. "But this time you were wearing a mask, a black mask over your eyes, and I knew it was you. In my dreams I'm starting to see. Something happened in that casino and maybe something good."

Chapter 16

Sheriff O'Madden parked his patrol car on the grass at the far end of the rutted parking area next to, he guessed, Reverend Jacob's black two-door Ford. And he wondered if he should have driven his civilian Ford pickup. The sheriff's badge insignia on the door with Elk County Sheriff and the mounted red light might be too intimidating. But this was an official call, of a sort, and on a Sunday afternoon, 3:00. He had predicted that the congregation had dispersed, and he'd find the reverend alone, and he did.

Reverend Jacob was attending the burlap snake sacks on the far side of the church. Sheriff O'Madden opened the vehicle door, stepped onto the grass, and closed the door.

Reverend Jacob walked over to greet the sheriff.

The sheriff met him halfway, extended his hand and said, "Sheriff O'Madden here."

"Reverend Jacob." The reverend was not intimidated in the least. The vehicle and uniform had an aura that the reverend penetrated. He was in touch with his sanctity.

"First. Whatever mission the Lord has sent you on, allow me to bless you. Kneel, Sheriff, and if you could take your trooper hat off."

The sheriff took off his hat and knelt.

The reverend placed his hands on his shoulders. "These hands, oh Lord, that have felt the evil of the vermin, that have held devils this blessed Sunday morning deliver your grace to this man of law so that he may subdue the evil forces that swarm us. May your legions of Archangels assist him in his battles. Arise."

The sheriff stood up. Placed his hat on awkwardly and looked at the reverend.

"And why am I graced with your visit?"

"I came here to see if you could help with solving the recent murders. I understand from Agent McClelan that you have psychic powers and that you helped solve a murder down south."

"Yes, I did. But I couldn't help him on this case." He looked up at the overcast sky. "There may be a storm brewing. Those rapidly moving clouds. Let's sit down on the steps of my mission church. The same place John and I talked. But I remember we had a bright sunny day."

They walked over to the church steps and sat down.

"Nice little church here. Nice setting," the sheriff said.

A howling wind blew over the church, rattled the leaves of poplar trees, and whipped the long grasses of the open fields.

"A good storm coming," the reverend said. "Most Signs Followers' churches are in rural areas or at least on the fringes of society. But Christ lived on the fringes of society. Do you know how many times Christ was in church? How many times you can count in the Bible?"

"I'm not a biblical scholar."

"Then I'll give you my times-in-church sermon. At the marriage feast, when he counseled the rabbis as a child, and when he drove out the money changers. His church was on the mountainsides and in the fields and in waters. Healing the sick and casting out demons. He was against all pomp and ceremony. Christ would embrace our humble church. And now, sheriff, enough of my sermon."

The sheriff reached in his pocket for the gambling token, placed it in the palm of his own hand. "I was given this by a man named

Coop, a mute hermit who lives in the Black River swamp. Coop may have found it at the first murder site. From what he tried to communicate to me, he may have witnessed the murder."

"Is Coop available…right now?"

"We'd have to find him. I know where his shack is."

"I'm feeling something already. But I don't want to touch the coin yet. Could we pick up Coop and drive to the first murder site?"

"I was hoping you would suggest that."

"Sheriff, psychic powers need every available advantage. Images only appear under the most intense conditions. We have an object which I can psychometrize, a possible witness, and the site of the crime. Let's go immediately."

"Psychometrize. You're acquainted with the term," the reverend said as they drove in the sheriff's patrol car to Coop's.

"Not exactly."

"Well, I'll explain. I can hold an object in my hands as I handle snakes. And allow the images from that object to emerge. While I handle the snakes, I see images. Not human. I see the devil in all her hideous splendor. And then I see her opposite—the angels. There is always this battle going on. But in this situation the original site is old by psychometry standards. So another human who may have witnessed the murder, the site itself, and the coin will be very powerful. I hope too powerful for Satan to overcome. Do you believe in Satan, Sheriff?"

The sheriff nodded and thought that there was something about the reverend's eyes that reminded him of that cold stare of Charles Manson.

"Someone said that the devil's biggest trap is confusing us to believe that she doesn't exist."

"I'll go along with that."

"I don't like to pass the collection plate around, but Agent McClelan made a generous contribution to Holiness Tabernacle Church. He passed the hat around and took up a collection at headquarters in Washington."

"I'll see what I can do when I get back to Elk headquarters. Keep the devil at bay."

The reverend smiled. "I'd appreciate it, Sheriff."

The sheriff turned off the blacktop and squeezed his patrol car onto a two-track. He switched on his headlights and clicked on the brights. The approaching storm of darkness and the overhead canopy of maples hung over the trail and closed in upon them. A flock of turkeys forced their right-of-way, and the sheriff stopped.

"Nine wild turkeys and still counting," the reverend said.

"They survived this harsh winter. Not only survived but thrived. We have a short turkey season now, by lottery. Coop survives on them along with his fishing and trapping."

"I'm looking forward to meeting him. 'The voice of one crying in the wilderness… Now John the Baptist wore a garment of camel's hair, and a leather girdle around his waist; and his food was locusts and wild honey.' That's Matthew, chapter 3, verse 4. I'll forego giving my baptism sermon. Have you ever been baptized, Sheriff?"

"This is it." The sheriff stopped in the middle of a clearing surrounded by immature white pines and scrub oak. He turned off the lights. "I would have never found Coop without the help of Lewis, a Native American friend who knows this wilderness and every creature in it. He said he'll lead us. He probably knows we're here and he'll guide us. See that trail?" He put on a white spotlight and aimed it at an opening in the woods. Both of them sat gazing over the hood at the deer trail. "That will take us to his shack."

The deer trail meandered through the woods, and they walked

easily until halted by a limb from an oak that had fallen over their path. They had to blaze their own trail to skirt around the branches. And on the other side of this brush pile stood Lewis, dressed in blue jeans, a red plaid shirt, and moccasins.

"Follow me," Lewis said.

"He's a man of few words," the sheriff whispered to the reverend. "I'll bring my axe the next time. If there is a next time."

As they neared the river, the footing became mucky. Distant, sharp flashes of lightning pierced the sky along with rolls of thunder.

The trail eventually rose onto solid ground, and at the top of a rise, Lewis stopped and stood on the edge of a clearing surrounded by large oaks.

The sheriff pointed his light at a shack on the other side. "That's it."

They walked across the clearing to the shack.

Lewis led them to the middle of the site and then sat on the ground.

"He should be close by. His evening meal." The sheriff pointed at the dying fire and the pile of turkey feathers and bones. The door was ajar. He grabbed the deer antler handle and opened the door. The shack was twelve feet square, made of rough-hewn cedar with a peaked roof covered with a multicolored patchwork of shingles. At the far end was a bed of white pine needles. At the foot, a pile of blankets. In one corner was a collection of ropes, wires, and fishing lines. "Turkey snares," the sheriff said.

They stepped back from the shack. "We can't holler for him," the sheriff said. "He can't hear us."

Lewis stood up and joined the sheriff and reverend in front of Coop's home. "When the butterflies arrive, I've seen them swarm around Coop. And he talks to them. And it seems like they answer."

"Butterflies? What next?" the sheriff said. "We can't wait for the butterflies to show up and assist in our interrogation. I've seen everything else. Why not talking butterflies."

"Let's circle the clearing. Walk around the edge of these oaks," the reverend said. "Make ourselves visible. He might see us."

"Maybe it would be best if I do the walking alone," the sheriff said. "You stay here."

Sheriff O'Madden stumbled onto a well-worn path that skirted the perimeter of the clearing, and he realized how Coop occupied his idle hours, tramping around the circle of his own hemisphere again and again and again, reliving the trauma of war in the vain effort to forget.

He walked around the path and returned where he had started at the hut. He stopped and then continued around again with the hope that Coop would see himself in an imitation of himself. Nothing. He walked past the shack again and nodded to the reverend, who was sitting on a stump by the smoldering fire.

Halfway around he heard a rustling of branches and leaves in an oak and looked up. Coop was comfortably perched in the crook of the tree, gnawing on a turkey bone. The sheriff remained rigid until Coop looked at him. He continued eating and spit out a bone that landed on the sheriff's hat. The sheriff took off his hat, patted it against his leg, and put it back on. He motioned for Coop to come down.

Looking at the reverend on the stump, Coop made the sign of the cross and then descended quickly and gracefully, stepping on the cross-boards nailed to the other side of the tree. When he reached the ground, he pointed at the reverend, who was standing in front of the shack.

The sheriff looked up at Coop, who was a head taller. He had on a straw hat that pushed his large ears out through thick white hair that draped over his shoulders. His long arms dangled at his sides and reached below his knees; his white beard touched his belt buckle. He was dressed in an old police uniform with pants that barely reached the top of his motorcycle boots.

Coop again pointed at the reverend and briskly walked over to the shack with the sheriff trailing him. He knelt in front of the reverend.

"So you've seen me give a blessing," the reverend said. "I felt your presence around Holy Tabernacle."

Coop took off his hat and bowed his head.

The reverend placed his hands on Coop's shoulders. "May the Lord who through me has cast out devils restore your hearing and speech. May you return again to the light of his glory. Devils begone." He placed his hand under Coop's chin and tilted his head up. Then he lifted his shoulders to raise him up.

Coop stood up and embraced the reverend. They held each other in silence until the reverend released his grasp, placed his hands on Coop's shoulders, and stared into his rheumy, blank gray eyes.

After a few minutes of quiet, the reverend said, "There's nothing there. Show him the coin, Sheriff, and he'll guess our plan."

The sheriff reached in his pocket, took out the coin, and, holding it in his fingers, raised it in front of Coop. Coop looked at the sheriff and turned to face the reverend. The reverend nodded and looked toward the middle of the site. Lewis had wandered off.

"It doesn't surprise me," the sheriff said. "He's like the wind. We'll find our way out of here with Coop's help."

※

The storm had moved in by the time they reached the first murder site. The sheriff parked on the periphery of an open tract. The reverend sat in the passenger seat. Coop sat in the back seat.

"This is it," the sheriff said.

"And where was the body found?"

"Next to that pine tree. It was lying on a bulldozer."

The sun had set. In the distance lightning streaked and illuminated the night sky.

They all stepped out of the patrol car.

Coop knew why he was here. In the deep recesses of his mind, he replayed that scene over and over again. It was the day, the day of the murder, and the rains had moved in after the death. Coop had remained in the shadows of the surrounding pines and lingered there until midnight after the rains abated, the storm passed, and a full moon beamed down upon the yellow bulldozer. He had walked across the clearing and up to the bulldozer and saw the gambling token lying on the running board. He picked it up without looking at the body, which lay on the other side of the tractor. The sky darkened again, and the rains returned and continued through the night, washing away all sign.

The sheriff pointed to a crucifix that marked the spot where the body had been found. The tombstone was a metal cross—two crowbars welded together, buried in cement. The family had placed it there to honor the victim, who was known for forging his own tools. A bluish glow beamed from its tip.

"Ah, he's still here. But fear not. That's St. Elmo's fire. You may even hear voices—mammals, birds. Strange sounds out here," the reverend said. "Sheriff, could you give me the coin?"

The sheriff handed him the token.

"And what was the victim's name?"

"Joe Salerno."

"Allow me to walk around this clearing, and you remain here

with Coop."

It had started to sprinkle. His boots dug into the soft earth. He slipped. Picked himself up and walked toward the glowing spike. In the distance there was a rumble of thunder and a sharp bolt of lightning.

"Saint Elmo's fire, guide me with your radiance; fill my mind with your visions." As he approached the glowing stake, he heard buzzing and hissing and he stopped.

"You can't drive me away, Satan. I have a token in my hand, and the sun, moon, and stars when they appear will sap your power as I will uncover this tomb of secrecy with this coin in my hand. The serpents that have slid through harmlessly and the blessings they have bestowed will overpower your darkness. Saint Erasmus of Formiae, guide me through the devil's tricks and give me the strength and courage to kneel before you and beg that you will enlighten my mind to Beelzebub's work."

As he approached the cross, a freezing blast of rotten air settled upon him. "You're still here, Joseph Salerno." He continued to walk toward the glowing cross and firmly clutched the coin.

Lightning struck a nearby tree, seared off a large limb, sparked down the trunk, and sizzled into the ground.

The reverend looked up as the limb cracked and thudded onto the earth. A bright white fire danced up and down the trunk of the oak. The rain pelted down harder, extinguished the fire, and spewed a dense pall of smoke over the clearing. Now quivering in front of the cross was the glowing outline of a human figure.

The sheriff and Coop rigidly stood in front of the patrol car on the periphery of the clearing, which was lighted like a playing field. They could only see the obscured dark outline of the reverend.

The apparition began to speak to the reverend in a deep guttural voice.
  "Release me," the figure said.
  "Who are you?"
  There was a long silence.
  "Are you Joseph Salerno?"
  "You have named me."
  "Who has committed this horrible abomination upon you?"
  "It is not for me to know or tell. My body fell from my soul as lightning cleaved the limb from the soul of the tree. But I remain here."
  "I will extract the devil's hold upon you." *He reached out to touch the apparition, his hands entering the glowing light in front of him.* *"May these hands dispel the vermin that have held you bondage and forgive you all your transgressions so that you may enter your just reward."*
  The luminescence in front of him began to spin and then broke up into smaller circles of light. Each ball of light further shattering into smaller spheres until only darkness remained.
  The reverend dropped to his knees and then lay prostrate upon the ground. He remained there clutching the token.

The rain stopped. The sky cleared, allowing the moon and stars to shine upon the clearing.

RAPTURE RIVER

The sheriff walked over to the prostrate reverend. He knelt and touched his shoulder. "Now I'd give you my blessing if I had one. But if I ever see this again, I'll become one of your converts, maybe. Everything has an explanation."

The reverend didn't respond.

The sheriff shook him, and he began to moan. He was wet with mud and grass.

"What happened out here? I've never seen anything like it."

A bat alighted on the reverend's hand, the hand he clutched the token with. It remained there for a few seconds, looked up blindly at the sheriff, and flew off.

Reverend Jacob lifted his head, looked at the sheriff, and said, "Good morning, bright outside."

"It's midnight. And tomorrow is just beginning."

The reverend sat up and looked at the steel cross.

"Do you know who murdered…"

"Yes," the reverend said. "Yes."

Chapter 17

Joyce and Josh were walking down the corridor of the Peace Gathering. They had lunch in the cafeteria, and she had asked him to sit in on her one o'clock class. He reluctantly accepted her invitation after she had told him that the class was reading Hawthorne's *The Scarlet Letter*.

They entered the class. Josh walked toward the back and sat near the window. Her students had not returned from lunch. She had on a black mandarin-collared Cherokee ribbon shirt. Red ribbons stitched on the front dangled freely a few inches from the hem.

As the seats were being filled by her students, she turned and wrote on the blackboard the letter A. On the back of her blouse was the letter A, of the same red ribbon as her shirt. She turned around, sat down at her desk, looked at Josh, and smiled.

Josh swallowed hard.

After the class filled and settled, she said, "Did everyone read their assignment? We now should be finished with the novel or at least close to it. But even if you didn't read it, you have some idea what's going on."

She stood up and turned around. And then faced the class again. "I wear the red letter on my back, but Hester Prynne wears it on the front of her blouse. Is there any difference?"

Billy raised his hand. "Yes, there is. If you wore it on your back, we wouldn't be aware of it when we talked to you. But if it's on the front of your blouse, then when someone talks to you, they probably look at the letter and wonder what it means. They might even avoid eye contact, and if they didn't know you, they might ask what it stands for."

"And I could say American…Native."

The class laughed.

"But I like your shirt," Billy said.

"My Cherokee ribbon shirt. And that's another story of us borrowing from our conquerors. Instead of leather dangling from our buckskin, we have ribbons dangling from our cotton shirts."

"And" Billy added, "horses weren't here until the Spanish brought them. And that's how we hunted buffalo."

"But let's get back to the subject. What does the A stand for?"

"Adultery," the class answered in unison.

"And what did it mean then, and what does it mean now? Didn't it have the same meaning then as it does now?"

The class was silent.

Joyce continued. "Attitudes were different then. And adultery carried a much heavier burden. But she was married to an older man, and he was absent. Our society doesn't forgive easily. So, is that what the story is about—forgiveness? And paying our debt? As we, or you, are paying your debt here? When you leave here should you wear the letter forever on your shirt and always be reminded of your guilt?"

"No!" Billy said.

"Good answer," Joyce said. "So, the books we studied this year—*Gulliver's Travels, The Lord of the Flies, The Scarlet Letter, The Lord of the Rings*. All these novels are about the interactions of the society in which a human being lives. Rules or laws are set down by the members of that particular society, and consequently you must obey them or else. You could be thrown out of that society or set up as an example and be paraded in front of everyone as Hester Prynne was."

The class moved in their seats, restless. Another student raised his hand. "We have already been given a scarlet letter. We just don't have it on."

"That's a brilliant answer," Joyce said.

"What do we have then?"

"Our red skin," blurted out Billy.

"I don't think that's true, but it may be to some people. Prejudice will always be there. Skin color alone is probably the biggest issue with prejudice. And what could be next? Maybe gender?

"Let's look at the attitudes of two men who lived three hundred years apart. I use the word attitude, but I could just as well have said prejudices. Alexander Pope was a poet and philosopher in England around the year 1700, and Colin Fletcher was a deep-thinking outdoorsman, a long-distance backpacker, around 2000. Colin walked, backpacked, the total length of California, one thousand miles, from Mexico to Oregon. Colin was an Englishman from Wales. No one, not even Native Americans, owns the deed to the house of nature. I'll read this from Colin Fletcher's book *River:*

Anyone who lives for long in any untouched landscape—especially in wide, stark, dramatic, primitive country—will find that, whether he recognizes it or not, the land becomes part of his religion. Probably forms its foundations. Ancient or modern man, it makes no difference. City dwellers, cut off from the land, naturally tend to disagree. Two and a half centuries ago, city dweller Alexander Pope wrote,

*   Lo, the poor Indian! Whose untutored mind*
*   Sees God in clouds, or hears him in the wind*

—though Pope did allow the poor Indian, through "simple nature...an humbler heaven." A modern tutored Indian might respond,

*   Lo, poor Alex Pope! Whose overtutored mind*
*   Cannot see God in clouds, or hear him in the wind.*

*   Anyway, for those in touch with the land, its substance reaches deep into their souls.*[2]

"Nature is a front for the Great Spirit," Josh said, "and I mean front in a good way." The class turned and looked at him.

---

[2] Fletcher, Colin. River: *One Man's Journey Down the Colorado, Source to Sea* (First Vintage Departures Edition, A Division of Penguin Random House May 1998), pp. 215-216. Fair Use determined. Used by permission.

Chapter 18

They drove in Joyce's red Prius to her grandmother's. Josh would sleep on the roll-out bed.

"Did you know that Hester's lover was a man of the cloth?" she asked as they drove up the Leelanau Peninsula.

"I read the novel. That he was a man of the cloth, I know. But at this moment I'm only concerned with getting to your grandmothers alive. You took that last curve at eighty. The speed limit is fifty-five."

"I know the cops. The Native American cops. We like speed, the freedom of it. It appeals to our nomadic nature. We can't shed our genetic past."

"Would you please slow down."

"Yes, Father."

"Josh."

"Joshua."

She decelerated to fifty. "Slow enough?"

"Yes, thank you."

"Maybe because I'm mad. The speed cheers me up. I want to forget."

"About us."

"No."

"About Lady Slipper. She died last night. My grandmother called me on her cell phone."

"I'm sorry. Why didn't you tell me?"
"I was overcast with grief and into...one of my trances."

Joyce drove down the gravel road to her grandmother's. Shanaya was standing on the porch waiting.

She parked, turned off the engine, and opened her door. He grabbed her shoulder. "Don't you want to take off the scarlet letter?"

"I'll change inside. If you're worried. She won't see it. Or... should I always wear it? Let it brand itself onto my back?" She smiled.

They entered the trailer.

Shanaya had laid the skunk in its sleeping basket and placed it on the kitchen table.

Joyce walked over to the table. "Lady Slipper. Your spirit is still here. I can feel you. All your warmth and affection. She has to be buried. We can bury her before it gets dark. There's a burial ground about twenty miles from here. I'll change these rags and put on my hiking boots."

Joyce placed Lady Slipper in the trunk of her car in the basket. She walked over to the utility shed, came back with a shovel, and set it alongside the skunk.

The burial ground was located in the center of the peninsula. And Joyce resumed her blatant violation of the speed limit. The erratic digital display of the speeding Prius shocked Josh—ninety-five— as he held onto the handle above his door window. "Hold it down." There was no answer. She appeared to be entering one of her trances while driving.

She turned off the two-lane blacktop onto a two-track, drove slowly for a short distance, and stopped. "This is as far as we can go."

They stepped out of the car. She opened the trunk, handed him the shovel, and picked up Lady Slipper in her bed.

She had not said one word while driving. She seemed possessed, again. So, he finally asked, "Why here?"

"I have no reason for being here. Except that I came to this hillock when I was a little girl. And I always remember this spot. When my grandmother took me here to bury my first pet—a stray dog. I don't know why we buried him here. Lewis told me that the summit is a fairy ring created by the circling wild mushrooms. They were part of my soul. They knew me and I knew them. We communicated. And so does this communication become enhanced at this spot because now I have two creatures buried here? I'll return here and meditate about the spirits of two deceased animals. This deer trail twists around these red pines to the burial site. The mark of their imprints will lead us up."

They reached the top—a bald spot encircled by red pines. Joyce set the basket down and stomped the ground. "Dig here."

Joyce lowered the basket into the crypt. "Now cover her with the earth."

He shoveled the dirt over the skunk.

The sun was beginning to set and descend below the surrounding red pines.

"Did you bring a flashlight?" Josh asked.

"No. We'll find our way out. I have good night vision."

He placed the last shovel of dirt on the mounded grave.

Joyce stood on the grave and jumped to flatten the mound.

"I'll do that," Josh said.

Joyce walked over to the side of the clearing, and Josh stomped on the grave. "We're done."

"All three of us." Her voice arose from the darkness.

"Where are you."

"I'm on this mossy boulder over here. I remember we buried my dog off to the side of this rock."

He walked in the direction of her voice. And sat down on the rock next to her. "Your hands are cold."

She said nothing but stared at the grave. He left her in her silence. She remained motionless for a few minutes and then looked up at the overhead passing clouds and the soft starlight falling upon the clearing.

"*Boozhoo.*" Hello. A voice rose from the woods.

"*Boozhoo, nijii.*" Hello, friend, Joyce answered.

She appeared out of the darkness, walked over to the freshly dug grave, and planted her bare feet on the mound of dirt. Her white hair snarled down over her shoulders. She was dressed in black cut-off jeans and a black sweatshirt. Through the dim light Josh could read "Ojibwa" across her chest. She was thin and the sweatshirt hung loosely beyond her waist. She continued her conversation with Joyce. At one point she spoke for a long time without Joyce interrupting her. When finished, Joyce asked her a question. She replied with a short answer and then began to sing and chant on the mound, moving her bare feet slightly over the earth, as if she intended to dance only on this little piece of dirt. She was into a prayer ritual for Joyce's dead skunk. Her dancing continued for a long time. Josh looked at his watch as she abruptly ended her movements, a half hour later. Joyce during this time clutched his hand. When she stopped her movements, she stood motionless and then turned around to the woods where she had come from, reentered the darkness, and disappeared into the red pines. He looked at his watch again, ten thirty.

Joyce sat there in silence. He finally said, "It might be best to call your grandmother on your cell phone."

"I know it won't work here," she said. "This whole area is a dead zone."

She stood up, holding his hand tightly, and led him over to the grave. The burial site was as silent as the surrounding woods. Were animals on the prowl at this late hour?

"Say a prayer, a Catholic prayer," she said.

He bowed his head. "Blessed are you, Lord God, maker of all living creatures. On the fifth and sixth days of creation, you called forth fish in the sea, birds in the air, and animals on the land. You inspired St. Francis to call all animals his brothers and sisters. Joyce and I ask you to bless this animal by the power of your love, enable it to live according to your plan. May we always praise you for your beauty in creation. Blessed are you, Lord our God, in your creatures. Amen."

They remained silent. Joyce held his hand firmly and led them out of the woods.

On the road she drove slowly, not anxious to return to her grandmother and her empty home, without Lady Slipper.

"Who was she?" Josh asked.

"She said she was the witch of the woods. I've heard of her. She roams the woods in this area. She is a product of the culture that thrives. We didn't even have a word for witch. But she is probably mentally unstable. I would guess a paranoid schizophrenic."

"What did she say?"

"She chanted Lady Slipper. And knew her name. But she could have heard her name from one of us as we climbed up the path. Although I can't remember using her name. But what surprised me was that she knew I was pregnant. She counted three hearts beating and said so and then said that I had two hearts. How could she know?"

"Did she say anything more about us—our future?"

"That would be convenient. Wouldn't it. Our very own fortune teller."

RAPTURE RIVER

They arrived at Joyce's grandmothers late. But a light was on in the kitchen, and he could see her silhouette in the den.

Shanaya stood up, walked to the door, and welcomed them. "I wish I would have gone with you," she said. "But I would only slow you down."

"We were slowed down because we were confronted by a shaman, a female shaman. She introduced herself as Barbara."

"Barbara. She calls herself a witch. But she's not," her grandmother said. "Only a name given to her by the inhabitants of the peninsula. I knew her when I was growing up. She's a few years younger than me. She's a half breed. Her mother was Ottawa, but her father was a Polish Catholic. I don't know where she got her mental illness from. She was institutionalized at the state mental hospital in Traverse City and was let out in the eighties when it was shut down. She was in for a long time. And she has roamed these woods since."

Barbara had faded into the shadows of the red pines, had followed the two along their path to the red car, had stood silently by and watched them drive the two-track to the paved road, had seen the lights zoom down the highway, had stood there as she saw the lights vanish. Now she was returning to the grave of the two creatures that she would commune with through the night. She reached the grave and began collecting branches and twigs and placing them in the middle of the clearing, in the firepit surrounded by the stones she had collected over the years. She reached in her jeans pocket and pulled out a lighter. She used the utensils of the modern. She stuffed some dried leaves under the branches and lit the fire. And the night breezes breathed onto the blaze and the flames roared forth. And she circled the hot radiance, her eyes glowing with intense light. She stepped to the crackling music of twigs and leaves. And she quickened her stride and broke away from the heat, enlarging her spiral. She stumbled and fell, her eyes averted to the blackness of the surrounding woods. And in that darkness was the light from the eyes of another creature, and the eyes rose from the ground and peered into the light. And then the whiteness slowly came upon her and offered its hand to help her up. She grasped Lewis's arm and slowly rose. She looked at him and nodded. He smiled. He was naked except for the polished bear stone of amethyst tied tightly around his neck with a leather thong. She squinted at the purpled sheen. And they embraced each other tightly until the heat from the fire singed. They backed away from the firepit and entered through the door of smoke the animal world of their ancestors. And they were greeted by a skunk and a dog who led them around the heat, and they stepped lightly to the silence and entered a deep trance.

"And she knew I was pregnant," Joyce said.

"That doesn't surprise me," her grandmother said. "Is there anything more important in your life at this moment. Is that all you think about?"

"That's what both of us think about," Josh said.

Chapter 19

Saint Peter the Fisherman Mission Church

Josh drove down the gravel road to Saint Peter the Fisherman Catholic Church and parked in a lot that ended smack in the middle of a coniferous forest. Sunday evening and the lot was empty. He had fished alone that afternoon, while Joyce and Ted remained sheltered in the cabin from the cold front that had moved in. Dark clouds whipped overhead as Michigan's fickle mitten warned that summer's rush was only a temporary fix.

The church lay deep within, hidden among tall white pines, about two blocks from the parking lot—a small chapel, seating about fifty, constructed with white pine and fieldstones harvested from the surrounding forest. It had been built in the early 50's by a log baron whose family was initially in the beaver trade and, when that dwindled, converted their resources to the timber industry.

Josh reached into his pocket. He had saved the spare key to the church. Locks don't change that often in the backwoods.

Sweetgrass was scattered thickly around two statues that flanked either side of the path to the church. On one side, St. Francis of Assisi, with a fawn, squirrel, and raccoon at his feet, his gaze fixed on a small bird perched on his finger. On the other side, Kateri Tekakwitha, Saint Kateri, the Lily of the Mohawks, holding a bouquet of lady slippers, at her feet clustered a mass of turtles.

He stood at the arched pine door entrance. Mounted above the door was a dove with outstretched wings. Braids of sweetgrass hung from its neck.

He inserted the key and unlocked the pine door, which flew open under its own weight. "Welcome home." Or was it the church that said, "Come in and stay for a while. Pray with me." His voice. The voice that transfigured him into a man of words, a preacher man. He stepped in, grasped the elk antler handle, and shut the door. The click of the latch resounded in the emptiness above the whistle of wind through the pines. Alone without a congregation. But maybe not. He and Joyce had a new soul emerging. He'd never go back to that old life. He lingered in the doorway. Off to his right was a large wooden bowl carved out of basswood lying on a pine stump—the baptismal font. On his right on the back wall hung a pine relief carving of St. Peter and his fishermen hauling in their nets. He read the caption: "Come ye after me, and I will make you fishers of men." He ran his fingers over the polished wood and then looked down the aisle of the empty chapel, walked up to the communion railing, and knelt in front of the altar. Off to the side was a statue of Mary chiseled out of a pine standing on a stump. Her eyes were closed and arms outstretched with a rosary laced with acorns dangling from her fingertips. At the base of the statue around her bare feet was a circle of unlit candles next to a box of matches. He stood, walked over to the statue, picked up the matches, lit a candle, and smudged out the match in the sand filling a turtle shell. The candle flickered in the cold, dark sanctuary. "I'll light two more." He picked up the matches again and lit two more candles. "For all three of us." The echo of his voice startled him. And he looked around the chapel to see if anyone was there. No, he was alone, but not alone. He'd never be alone again. And he loved this new life.

He returned to the railing, knelt, bowed his head, and pressed his palms together. He prayed until he heard a crack at the door. A wind-whipped branch? The howl of a coyote gave him pause to remain and meditate before joining Joyce and Ted and Molly back at the cabin.

The door blew open, letting in a cold draft. Josh turned around. Joyce's silhouette appeared in the dim light of the candles. She shut the door against the wind, walked down the aisle to the communion railing, and knelt next to him.

"How'd you get here?" he whispered.

"Ted's jeep. We were both worried. I guessed you came here. A shelter from the storm. Your key still works."

"Nothing changes out here," he said.

"Nothing spiritual," Joyce replied. "That most important part of us is always in a state of flux. The same key that opened your spirit before will open it now."

"Some of it will always be there," Josh said.

"Mine will always be in me. Nature opens my spirit world. At least we can agree on a spirit world. It's a path for both of us. A spirit with arms outstretched that will embrace us." She looked at the three candles off to the side under the statue. She stood and walked over to the candles, picked up the candle snuffer, a small clamshell wired to a hickory stick, and extinguished a candle. She walked back to the railing, knelt, and looked at the altar.

"Why'd you do that?"

"There are now only two."

"Only two?"

"Yes, only two. You and me." She placed her hand on his shoulder. "Our new spirit is no more. And I think Molly was the first to know. When you were away last week at the Social Services meeting, Molly slept on the foot of our bed, and when I awoke she looked at me in a way that she knew something was gone and began whimpering. Molly and I are close, closer than you realize. I realize now what she went through when she had to give up her litter, four puppies, to some unknown buyer. How horrible that was for her. I remember how she held close to me in her sorrow. She will have no more of her own but senses life when it's beginning in another—one of her sisters. She began whining, clinging to me like a vine around a tree. I had never heard a sound like that from any animal. I lay there on the bed for hours, her paws wrapped around me, while she licked away my tears. My child was gone, but the infant's spirit clung to me. And Molly felt the presence of that spirit."

"Why didn't you tell me sooner?" he said.

"I couldn't get myself to tell you. I knew how you'd take it."

Josh picked up a Bible and slammed it on the floor, its sharp echo filling the empty church.

"No," she said. "No. Both of us share this, and it will always be a part of us. I'll share myself with you as Molly gave herself to me. Molly assisted in my healing, and now we must heal each other. Nature was my chapel.

"I cared for myself as best I could that morning. But I decided to end this ending in the stream. The day was warm, and Molly and I got into Ted's jeep and drove to the river, the deep pool below McKinnan's Bend.

"The noonday summer sun's reflection off the river blinded us as we walked to the river. Molly pressed against my thigh, licking my hand and nibbling at my fingers. On the bank I shed all my clothes in a pile and walked bare to the river, with Molly guiding me to the water. I half expected her to remain on the bank as she does with you and Ted, but she felt the anguish of my needs. I breathed in deep the wild cedar scent from the surrounding trees, splashed into the deep water, and Molly dove in after me. She stayed next to me as we treaded water. Both of us swam upstream, pushing against the current. I dove under and Molly plunged down with me, the departing soul still embracing my spirit. She held close as we neared the gravelly bottom and then nudged her nose under my chin, attempting to lift me up, fearing for my life. I surfaced and she rose with me and began swimming around me, circling me again and again. After a time, we began to play—a riot of splashing and laughing and barking. We played until both of us were, well, dog-tired. And suddenly Molly stopped, swam toward the shore, climbed the bank, and sat by my pile of clothes. She knew I was, well, healed. I joined her on the bank, dressed, and we sat for hours clinging to each other and staring at the current until the sun set. And I sensed the final release of my unborn's spirit into the hand of the Great Spirit. And I was relieved and grateful."

"That was beautiful," Josh said. "Is this a ritual that Native Americans follow?'

"No, I follow this," placing her hand over her heart. "Too many rituals, laws, ceremonies. We have no churchy liturgy. Our elders preserve our rituals, which is good, but even they become too rigid. But what they do teach is to follow nature, which surrounds us. See the spirit in nature. I bow to the spirit in nature and my own instincts, allowing my spirit to be carried wherever she wishes to go. Maybe we are blessed that we don't have a thick book guiding us. This isn't the only sanctified spot in these woods. A cathedral, a forest cathedral, of the Great Spirit is outside these mission doors. A temple of the Holy Spirit, the Great Spirit."

"That sounds like Ted," Josh said.

"It is," Joyce replied. "You may have learned that from Ted, but you don't feel it."

"I'm a slow learner."

"And you will in time feel it."

Joyce stood up and genuflected in front of the altar, walked over to the statue of Saint Katerina, the Lily of the Mohawks, against the wall opposite the candles. Both of her hands were raised as were the hands of the statue on the opposite side. But cupped in one hand was a shell, in the other, a feather from a red-tailed hawk. Lying at her feet was a turtle shell holding a plastic bag of sage and a pack of matches.

She opened the sage and scattered the leaves into the abalone shell, picked up a match, and lit the sage. She took the feather from the hand of the statue and fanned the flames. Holding the shell in both hands, she walked back and set the shell on the floor in front of the altar. They stared at the mural behind the altar—St. John the Baptist in the Jordan River pouring water over the head of a new convert.

They knelt in silence, the rain tinkling on the tin roof, the wind humming through the trees, the candles flickering, the embers of sage glowing, and two hearts beating.

Part 2

Chapter 20

Ted held onto his walking stick and hefted himself up onto the cedar bank, Molly already resting against a fallen cedar. He'd rest here and wait for the hatches of Brown Drake. "Litobrancha recurvata," he said, his crackling voice rising above the bubbling river. He sat down on the cedar tree. *You didn't last as long as I have. I think back to the day you stood straight and tall, like me, seventy years ago, and I was in my teens. And now they call them terrible teens. Not me, back then. Up here was like heaven, freedom from that hell in the cast house in the prison of the steel mill.* He rested his pole against a sapling, extended his legs, slid down onto the ground, and looked up through breaks in the overhead canopy at the circling vultures. "I hope they're not for me." He smiled. "Maybe my welcoming. Hey, you're late. No—too early. Molly, you protect me from their evil wrath." He sat and rested his head against the cedar, dozed off, and drifted into dreamland with Molly stretched out beside him.

Crow flew down and perched on a cedar branch just above Molly, the limb bending under the crow's weight and brushing against Molly's back. Molly sprang up on all fours, geared up for flight or fight, her tail upright. She looked above at Crow and shook her head. "Oh, it's only you again."

"I'm sorry," said Crow, "didn't mean to wake you, just scratch your back."

"I'm sure," said Molly. "Now, don't 'caw' and wake Ted and end his trance and us along with it. So, I know you want another meetin. Go gather up Squirrel, Rabbit, Woodchuck, Owl, and whoever you wants to come."

"Will do," said Crow. "You are the only domesticated creature in our pack. I'm happy you showed up with Ted. And his dreaming opens our gateway. How you do that?"

"I don't know. It's magic. But are we real or ain't we real. Only in a dream, maybe. But I feel real. So make haste while we still around. Crow, let's have our wilderness hall gathering. Call in all who dwell in this river valley to our camp."

"Should I invite Bear?" asked Crow. "And the three cubs?"

"No. With all this stalking going on, humans and bear don't mix."

Crow flew off and landed high on an oak and cawed the congregation together.

Another lazy day for Molly, but she'd welcome that and simply enjoy the warm spring evening. Her life had been so full since Joyce, her mistress, joined into their cabin with her man, Josh. And how their presence opened the spirit world and gave them the way to steal into the spirit world of humans, a mystery. But why did humans have such a time with relationships? Damn. Why can't we just talk to them directly and not only through their dreams? But we'll get there.

RAPTURE RIVER

Someday we'll get there before it's too late. And Ted now slower but the best master that an animal may desire. And around her the other animals began to congregate as Ted drifted deeper into slumber, enabling their presence. Molly knew she was the slipstream, the current into Ted's dreams. And the Kingdom gathered.

Crow flew down from her perch and landed on the limb above Molly. "Me be the judge," said Crow.

"No way," said Squirrel. "Just because you dressed in black and land above Molly don't mean you rule this land."

"This be our hour to meet and must be order," said Crow.

"Order meat," said Ruffed Grouse. "I'm a delicacy and I don't desire a connoisseur's plate adorned with my spiritual presence. We are constrained by the meager time we share together."

"You, high-class bird," said Groundhog, burrowing his head above his den. "Where you get such high-class talk. This pun talk gonna wear me out."

"She flaunts her speech like she wear her plumage," said Mourning Dove.

"Let's get out of this foolishness," said Skunk, peeking around a tree.

"I knew you was here," said Turkey. "You are unmistakable and without a doubt the most advanced, aromatic creature on the face of the earth. And humans, some humans, would call you a turkey."

Skunk held his head down.

"She's the turkey and should apologize," said Badger.

"You don't have to be sorry," said Skunk. "I know my attractive powers."

"Now," said Crow, shaking the limb she perched on. "I alighted on this limb to bring order to this meeting before the light goes out, the sun sets. So let's keep talk on our two lovers."

"Let's give Rabbit the ground," said Owl. "She's the expert on intimacy."

A chorus of chirping, barking, chattering, purring, clucking, and squeaking applauded Rabbit as she hopped forward, and the animals circled around her.

"Bow to the queen," said Beaver. "She has a tale to tell."

"But not a flat tale like your tail," said Snake. "A long tail like mine that will whip you into attention."

"Snake give you a tension which is unbearable," said Mouse. "Especially when she come to eat you."

"Good no bear here. All here are unbearable to bear a bear," said Mockingbird.

"Mockingbird, you stay quiet," said Crow. "Any minute now you caw like me, and we don't know who sings. Proceed, Queen Rabbit. You the mating queen."

"Yes, I is," said Rabbit. "And I have the population of my den rabbit hole to prove it. Y'all know that. I seen um in the river. And it be the most incongruous, voluptuous affair I have ever witnessed."

"What you mean by incog volup," said Squirrel.

"It means you making love like mad in a very odd place. See what I tell you. She wade upstream after the fish swims out of her net, and they sit on a log getting ready to mate, playing before."

"Foreplay, they call that," said Mockingbird.

"Thank you, Mockingbird," said Rabbit. "And when they all excited, they go in the middle of the stream, and he tries to net her in his net, and she just laughs; they hold onto each other and they matin' for a long time. And the only thing that breaks them apart is Osprey. She dives into the river for *her evening meal of trout. And they just standing there, and that water splashing across the river, wettin them, and they break apart from their sex orgy. And then after that orgy of water, Joyce just stand in a spell. And Father Josh. Wait now, I guess he no Father no more. Let's see. I guess he maybe be Lover Josh. And when walking out of the river into the brambles, I hear their hearts beatin, and his the loudest."*

Ted turned his head on the log. "Getting dark, Molly. Get going to the bar."

Chapter 21

The bar was located in Vanderbilt, ten miles from the Black River. The village consisted of a gas station, a diner, and two churches, one Baptist, the other Catholic. Vanderbilt held the record for the coldest temperature ever recorded in Michigan, minus fifty-one degrees Fahrenheit in 1934. Once that was recorded, whether exactly correct or not, the inhabitants in the immediate vicinity had no doubt that they lived in, yes, the coldest spot ever in the state, no question.

The bar, the Cold Spot, was built of fieldstones. The local fishermen simply called it the Trout Bar. A single pine tree extended the length of the bar and was claimed by the current owner to be the longest single-cut pine bar in the state. But claims like this only reinforced the preposterous length of the fish that inhabited the Black—fish stories that had no limit to their enormity and length, as that record cold day had no equal.

When Ted entered, two fishermen were sitting in front of the fire.

"Where's Molly?" the bartender said.

"Left her in the Jeep. Didn't know who'd be in here."

"She's always welcome."

"I'll get her," Ted said.

Ted opened the Jeep door, and Molly jumped down onto the ground, the slipstream of Ted's brain waves lingering. *Well, I wondered when he'd get back here and let me in, she thought. She walked by his side without any leash and entered the bar ahead of him. Only two men at a table, the barkeep, and no other dogs leashed to the bar. Her master always would forego the leash. Her privilege as a well-behaved dog. I'll get the attention that they give the only female in the company of men.*

Along the front of the bar were fastened a few coat hooks where customers leashed their dogs. But Ted never had to leash Molly because Molly had table manners. She didn't beg but accepted offerings graciously and welcomed petting. Attention she loved, and the occasional bite that was tossed her way, but she never mooched. Ever since Ted's wife passed away, he'd driven there from his cabin to escape a lonely night and catch the fisherman talk about the spawning season in the fall and the hatches in spring. During May the talk became alive with hatching mayflies. In the fall when the spawning season peaked, a serious mood of non-interference surfaced. The spreads area, the spawning grounds on the Black, was listed as off-limits amongst the locals, and since it coursed through the private property of Black River Ranch, easy access was not possible. The Black River Ranch was guarding their spawning beds. *Never make that land public because the general population will not understand the importance of the breeding grounds. The brook trout will survive long after all are gone. And the Great Spirit wants them to flourish.*

"Hey, Molly." The barkeep, Connell, leaned over the bar to greet her.

Molly wagged her tail and softly barked her welcome.

"Got one to tell you," Connell said, nodding to Ted. Connell picked Ted's favorite mug and filled it with beer from the tap and placed it in front of Ted. He leaned over toward Ted. "Two guys by the end table over there. One guy is a federal marshal. And the other guy is—the one wearing the kilt—get this…a professor from

Edinburgh University in Scotland, doing research on Hemingway. He's on his way to the Big Two-Hearted and Fox rivers in the Upper Peninsula but stopped over by the Black because the name comes up in Hemingway's stories and his letters. I told him about you and if he wants to know anything about fishing, there's no one who knows more. Want me to introduce you?"

"Sure," Ted said.

"Hey, Oliver," Connell yelled over the empty bar, "this is the guy, Ted, that I was telling you about. Knows all about the Black."

"By golly, Sir Ted, come join us," Oliver said. "Cheers."

Ted slid off the bar stool and walked over to the table, Molly following him.

"This feels like home," Oliver said. "Our country pubs are set up the same way. With leash hooks on the bar. What's her name?"

"Molly," replied Ted.

"Molly," Oliver said, "a proper British name. And that Connell. A gentleman of such high taste in literature. And the leash hooks are there from the Englishman Connell. And he informed me how he grew up in Haworth and his father owned a country pub and talking about the novel *Wuthering Heights*."

Molly sat on her hind legs between Oliver and Ted. She stared up at Oliver, so tall, fascinated by his accent and full head of disheveled red hair, which fell onto his chest.

"Such a grand animal," Oliver said as he bent down to pet Molly, his red hair brushing over Molly. "And that look of hers, those eyes. She is immediately a female. I feel her. Her gentleness and uncanny, mysterious aura."

"Aura?"

"Yes, Sir Ted. Her soul, Sir Ted. She thinks but does she talk?"

"Not yet," Ted said.

"But she has intentions in that regard, I would conjecture."

"If she does I hope without an accent. On my phone I had to

decode the jabber from a credit card that added up to a heap of garbage. Could have been a message from Mars."

"Well, you wouldn't mind a wee bit of a Scottish accent."

"Like yours. That's fine. Would it be okay with you, Molly?"

Molly nodded.

"See, she totally concurs. A golden Labrador with a Scottish accent."

"She loves everyone," Ted said. "And how long do you plan on staying in Vanderbilt?"

"A few days."

"Ever fly-fish?"

"Never."

"I could take you out. Fix you up with waders and equipment."

"That would be splendid."

Oliver turned to John McClelan. "This is John. Or to be proper—Federal Marshal John McClelan. An interesting gentleman. And might I add a very gracious hoist. The Black has some problems, I gather."

Molly looked up at Oliver, her dream time with Ted not fully drowned out. Not any problems caused by us animals. Not even my master. She looked about her and could see the interference with nature. I can hear the explosions under the ground and can sniff the oil and gas before it reaches the surface. I can see the change in the fishing. Is that quivering ground causing Ted to return to the cabin with an empty creel? I feel the quiver and you don't.

Ted extended his hand to John. "I've heard you were here, and I wondered how it was going."

"Fishing and oil don't mix. Very well at least. We're at a standstill right now and will remain there until I get some headway with Reverend Jacob. I've been told that he knows who the murderer is or has an assumption—a definite assumption of guilt, probably a member of his church. I guess as a priest he could not disclose the identity of whoever might have committed the murder."

"He's just a serpent handler, not a Catholic priest," Ted said.

"But he is a dedicated cleric," John said. "I've never met a priest who violated the confessional seal. And he calls himself a priest. It all depends on how dedicated and the density of your belief. Either hot or cold. If I were to go to confession, he would be my first choice."

"My first choice would be Joshua. Some give into the rumor that he's a fallen priest. But then I still see the priest in him," Ted said. "It clings to him more than he clings to it. You can take the boy out of the Catholic Church, but you can't take the Catholicism out of the boy. It's like a dog, like Molly, always there by your side, no matter what. But I'd go to Josh, Father Joshua, before I'd go to a snake charmer."

"Reverend Jacob could scare the devil away," John said. "If there is such a thing as a devil? So what's your take on this, Oliver?"

"I'm an atheist," Oliver said. "But in a way it's a contradiction. I see others who believe in a god, but I deny that what they believe does not exist. If I were a pure nonbeliever, I would have to live in a place where no one believed."

Molly was very attentive to his accent as he said, "I should have been a dog and suddenly transformed into a human and then I would have been pure in my beliefs."

"No one can be pure in his beliefs," John said. "Who is guilty of these murders? And what were the motives? If there were any motives. At least, that we can call motives."

"You think too deep, deep as Black River mud," Ted said, "and as smelly."

"To change the subject," Oliver said, alerted to the tension, "I welcome your invitation to fly-fish one of Hemingway's streams. Honesty surfaces from the deep river within you."

Molly set her paw on Ted's knee.

"She knows her master," Oliver said. "And I respect her for that. If she could only talk."

"Joyce talks to her. They're real close. Joyce assisted at her first delivery of four puppies. And they bonded."

"Joyce?"

"An Ojibwa girl. Well, girl, woman who sleeps overnight at my cabin."

"Native American. I didn't realize how much depth of cultural interaction I would be exposed to here. It becomes more fascinating by the minute."

Connell, beer pitcher in hand, walked over to the table. "Any refills?"

Oliver lifted his mug. "Cheers." He set it on the table and Connell refilled.

"First I've heard 'cheers' in many a year." Connell set the pitcher in the middle of the table. "You boys don't guzzle like Oliver. Must be thirsty after all that travel."

"That I am," Oliver said. "From the airport to here in my rented gas-guzzling SUV. Fluid. We all run on fluid." He sipped the foam off his mug. "'We all need water, new water.' Those words spoken by your American naturalist Henry David Thoreau. 'New water. A man's life should be as fresh as a river. It should be the same channel but a new water every minute.'"

"Say again," Ted said.

"In another way, Thoreau wrote, 'Life in us is like water in a river.'"

"That I see," Ted said.

"And when we go fishing together, Ted, what are we after? Mr. Thoreau said, 'Men go fishing without knowing it is fish they are after.'"

Ted sipped from his mug, set it on the table, and looked across at John and Oliver. "So what was Hemingway after? After something else. That he never caught."

"That's what I'm after," Oliver said. "But it…maybe will always elude me. Some may say that an old crackpot from Scotland showed up looking for Hemingway. The man was a word magician. And writers have always been after his magic, never to catch it. But it's intriguing. I researched Hemingway for nigh twenty years. And I have the feeling that I'll learn more in the short time I'm here. We know Hemingway fished the Black, from his letters. And get this." He reached in his shirt pocket and pulled out a note. "Recently a four-page, handwritten letter of Hemingway's was auctioned off for $237,055. He signed it Ernie."

"Say again," Connell yelled over the bar. He walked over to Oliver. "Let me see." He read the note. "Auctioned by Nate D. Sanders, $237,055. Why would anyone?"

"Hemingway was a mystery. And owning that letter gets one closer to his mystery. And the story of his love life and several wives. He never could be satisfied. Always after the next adventure, whether it be a fish or a companion."

"There's a world out there outside of books," John interrupted.

"But," Oliver said, "I can't see myself in that river. You'll stay close. Will you, Ted?"

"Of course," Ted said, "and Molly will be there with us."

Molly brushed against Ted's knee.

"Sounds like the same story the river is telling again," Ted said.

"Telling what, Sir Ted?" asked Oliver.

"There's Josh…let's say former Catholic priest who loves the Black and loves Joyce. Father Josh…there I go again. He's not a priest anymore but I call him my confessor. Once a priest, always a priest. Stick around and we'll finish this evening till the wee hours of the morning."

Chapter 22

"Observe," Oliver said, "up the stream."

"Quiet," whispered Ted.

A turtle floated downstream on the current as Ted and Oliver sat on the bank threading their line through the guides of their rods, Molly at their side. Caught in an eddy around a boulder, the turtle flipped upside down. It righted itself by paddling frantically, using all four feet as flippers or rudders, and then with its head held upright glided with the pull of the river, enjoying the passing scenery and searching for a safe landing. It spun in a whirlpool as it passed Oliver and Ted on the bank, plunged under, and surfaced downstream.

"Must have seen us," Ted said. He picked a yellowish-brown grasshopper off a blade of river grass and pitched it onto the current. It twirled with the current, struggling to break away without success, and was sucked in by a trout.

"Now that was a big fish," Ted said. "He just rolled above the surface for his meal."

"And I experienced a grasshopper from a river Hemingway waded in. My day is complete."

"We're just getting started."

RAPTURE RIVER

Molly followed them along the bank. Ted's fly-fishing instruction reached the peak of success when Oliver caught a twelve-inch brook trout on a Brown Drake dry fly. Oliver had cast, hooked, and netted the brookie.

"That's a beautiful fish," Ted said.

"I…I…I." Oliver was speechless.

"Let's go to the riverside, and I'll show you how to clean a trout." Ted sat on a log bank-side, and Oliver knelt beside him on the grass. Ted made a slit from the anus to the gills, grasped the gills, and ripped out the insides. He flipped the offal along the stream's edge. "That turtle will have his meal. Now you only have to clean the kidneys out. That blood along the backbone. You can do it with your fingers, but I always carry a toothbrush to make it clean. A big trout like this. And this is a big trout. These bones along the backbone can be sharp," and he brushed away the blood. "There now, clean. Lean toward me. This won't hurt." Ted smudged Oliver's forehead with his bloody index finger. "My father did that to me after I shot my first deer. Of course, with a deer. It's your first wild animal. We'll do it with a fish. Now your first fish. Leave it there until it dries and wears off. The hunter's ritual."

"My God in heaven. I've been baptized. I'm a believer, in nature and its rituals."

Ted washed the fish, splashing it back and forth in the river, and set it on the river grass. "Take a picture. That cell phone in your shirt pocket. I never carry mine. It sits in my cabin. Maybe ringing now. Get in closer so you can pick up those blue halos around red dots."

"I see, I see," Oliver said.

Molly barked.

"Where you been, girl," Ted said.

She ran toward them, stopped, and then ran a few feet back along the deer trail. Stopped and barked again.

"She wants us to follow her," Ted said.

Ted and Oliver laid their rods against a pine stump and set out on the deer trail. The land rolled away from the river, rising to solid ground and then dipping into mucky traps of still water, reservoirs for the rain. Scattered scrub, jack pine, and quaking aspen leaned over the deer trail. Molly, as the deer, glided along through this tunnel of brush while Ted and Oliver slaved away to keep pace, Ted feeling his way with his walking stick, Oliver directly behind.

Molly scurried ahead, stopped at the peak of a rise, and wandered off the trail. "I lost her," Ted said.

"And any minute now I shall be a loss, joining Beelzebub, along with his or her gracious flies," Oliver said. "If I sink any further, I'll be over my knees."

"You're not quite over your ankles yet. Pull yourself out one foot at a time. Don't worry about the sucking sound. No devils under this earth. They're down deeper."

"Thank you, Sir Ted, such gracious advice." He climbed out of the gully and joined Ted on the crest of a hillock.

"There she is, pointing down that gully off to her side." They walked over to Molly and were paralyzed by the sight at the bottom of the gully.

A slight breeze picked up, carrying a stench of decomposing flesh, human flesh, and the shock of that stink forced them to cover their faces with the sleeves of their shirts.

Oliver turned his head and gasped for air. He looked back down the gully. "This is not a ghostly apparition but the corpse of a human being, advanced into decay."

"I was here five days ago with Molly," Ted said, "so it could be a few days old. Native American. Looks like old Bill Catches. He was getting into some dementia. Could be murder but maybe he simply took off his blanket and let nature in. Call it what you will. Passing on from the disease of a long life assisted by the Great Spirit. Great Spirit-assisted passing on, not physician-assisted suicide. We need

RAPTURE RIVER

new words for all this," and he knelt down next to Molly, bracing himself on his cane. He hugged Molly and she leaned against him, licking his hand. "Wish Josh were here. He'd have the right words. But I can try. In the name of the Great Spirit, he departed against the earth, his home. Finally, he found his peace on a riverbank of the Great Spirit. Amen." He bowed his head, folded his hands, and prayed silently.

Oliver remained standing and took his cell phone out of his pocket.

"Might not work here," Ted said. "A dead zone. But call in to 911 and see what happens."

"Dead," Oliver said.

"With all these cell phone towers. Smoke signals were more reliable. We'll have to escape this swamp and get near my place before we get through to Sheriff Mad."

Smoke had shrouded Bill Catches as he hobbled down the hillside. He could've driven his daughter's Ford, but he rode his mule on the deer path through the woods, his mule from so many years ago. How many? Years? No matter. A question with no answer. He couldn't remember. When he looked in the mirror this morning, he didn't know who he saw. Was it him? Who was him? He didn't have an idea who that image was. To arise every day and be fed and set in front of a TV, which is nothing but a flat screen that wouldn't give him any idea who he was in this new digital world.

No computer. No cell phone. He attempted to learn com-

puters but simply gave up and quit. Couldn't catch on, but he could catch a fish. So few had ever even fished. High above, an eagle circled and then he didn't see the eagle. Was it the cold setting in? Something new stealing his mind? If there was anything left to steal. He looked back up the hill. Was it his daughter's Ford or his mule on the hilltop? He set one foot down after another. Only conscious that he was moving down, down, down. And he was riding the mule down the hillside with his dog at his side. He hadn't seen her in over seventy years. "Come along, Drummer." His voice startled him. Little Drummer he'd called her at first, then just plain Drummer. She'd been his best dog. Was she gone now? What was gone? Not here? Where? Draped over the mule was his blanket, or was it simply hanging over his shoulder and tied down with deer hide against his own middle? He tripped on a log and plunged into a bed of pine needles. Stunned, he stood and brushed off his flannel shirt and jeans. No dog, no mule. And on he walked alone with his blanket along the bottom of the hill until he heard the river. He stopped, walked down into a gully, and sat. He untied his blanket and wrapped it over his crossed knees. At one time he could run down, fly down these hills. Now, after this night, he'd fly up and soar with the hawks he revered during his living time.

Chapter 23

Josh unlocked the door to Saint Peter the Fisherman Catholic Church. He stepped into the darkness. The sun shining through an oval skylight fell upon the altar, enclosing it in a perfect circle.

He walked down the aisle, genuflected in front of the altar, and opened the package he carried. He unrolled a white linen cover, smoothed it over the altar's table, and set a black box with the remains of Bill Catches in the center.

"You back home now, Father Josh," said a voice from the rear. "I watch you walk up. I was here before the sun. Jedidiah, it's me, Father Josh," he added as he walked down the aisle.

"No more 'Father.'"

"Just for today. Before the day is done, I want confession."

"Okay, okay. I had to pull many strings to minister this funeral with Reverend Jacob, but Joyce insisted."

"You know why. After you left the Church, one of Bill's great-grandchildren took him to Reverend Jacob's church, and he felt renewed, almost cured. There's a feeling that Bill is Joyce's grandfather. Shanaya made Joyce go to you to get Reverend Jacob into his funeral service, and now Joyce knows the truth."

"That makes sense."

"This hilltop and church will be overflowing this morning, and when we spread his ashes in the river, more humans than fish in the river."

"When I told Sheriff Mad I would be the one to scatter his ashes in the river, he cautioned me that ashes can only be spread on private property."

"This is our private property. Our river. This is ours. They call it state land. Tell the sheriff to let the wind blow caution away."

"You're right."

"Shanaya made me usher. On this side in the front row Shanaya, Joyce, and family; in the second row Ted with Molly and Oliver. On the other side Sheriff Mad with Marshal Boy and the military guard. The flag for his war service will be presented to Shanaya. Back seats will fill up. Some will be sitting in the aisle."

After parking near the river, Reverend Jacob had tramped along the river on a deer trail headed for the hilltop church funeral. He'd follow Bill's footsteps, if not walk in his moccasins. Maybe touch a part of him near the river. And the river whispered Bill's life story pouring out and streaming through Reverend Jacob, and he was crying then laughing at the same time, his emotions unable to keep pace with his thoughts. His black cowboy boots sank into the muck and jolted him into the now. He looked at the trail rising to the church and dug his mud-splattered boots into the zigzagging trail winding up. At the crest he stopped and gazed over the throng. The sight of this black, lean figure with disheveled white hair set a murmur rippling through the crowd. Reverend Jacob gazed over the crowd of natives sitting cross-legged on the earth and pressed his way into the crowd, which leaned aside, creating a clear path to the church entrance, the door held open by Lewis. He stomped on the wooden floor as he passed Lewis, and the congregation turned around to this white-haired, black apparition in the doorway. "Good day, fellow mourners, on this celebration of Bill Catches' life," he said.

"Good morning, Reverend," repeated the congregation.

Those seated in the aisle stood to make way for the reverend as he felt his way to the altar. He knelt before the altar and said, "May God bless our service for Bill Catches," and he walked around the altar to face the congregation.

He gazed over the congregation. "What is heaven? Where is heaven? Where is the Happy Hunting Ground? Is it right here and we can't see it? There is a Native American legend that claims we can see heaven in the night sky—in the Milky Way. And all the sparkling lights are the souls of the departed—going on forever and ever. But the pathway to the Milky Way, if you look close enough in the night sky, has a break in it, a fork, and you must cross a bridge to get to the other side. Guarding that bridge are all the dogs you owned in your lifetime. If you treated your dogs well in your lifetime, you will be guided across by your dogs. If not…"

Molly stood on all fours and barked loudly.

The congregation squirmed in their seats, some standing. From the back row came "Molly knows, Preacher, Molly knows."

At the sound of her name, Molly, in the middle of the front aisle, turned toward her caller and barked again. Laughter broke out, the congregation standing and clapping. An altar boy with a hawk feather fanned the bowl of burning sage at the feet of Mary's statue, and smoke curled over the congregation.

Ted petted Molly's back as she clung to his side.

Preacher Jacob raised his hands and slowly lowered them, touching the black box, the congregation quieting.

He hesitated, staring at the black box and conjuring the spirit of Bill Catches. The box began to quiver, whether from Reverend Jacob's own conjuring or from the spirit within the box. "He is with us. And he will always be with us. This morning, I walked in his footsteps along the river, and the river spoke to me. Did I walk in his moccasins?"

"No, Preacher," shouted Lewis from the church's doorway. "You followed his footsteps." The crowd from the surrounding churchyard began pushing their way in when they heard Lewis's voice.

"Come into the Lord's house," Preacher called out to Lewis. "Fill around the altar. Hang from the overhead log beams if need be." And they tumbled in. "Remember this is not the Lord's only house. His home is out there in the swamps, forests, cities, mansions, slum huts, banks, bars, gambling casinos, battlefields, cornfields, prisons, mental hospitals, everywhere. But I feel him here on this sacred morning. Do you feel the Lord this morning?"

"Preacher Jacob, he's right next to me. If I can't see him, I feel him," cried out a squatting man in the aisle.

"And his presence was sure when Bill attended the Signs Followers' chapel," the reverend continued. "Bill was set free from his mental dungeon by channeling through the poison of vermin, without touching, without handling the serpents. The mere presence of their venom untangled the knots of his mind. And he felt alive. We are not given to know his thoughts as he descended the hill to his final moments on earth. His family confessed that he mumbled about his favorite dog, Drummer, his last few days."

In the front row Molly wrapped her paw around Ted's arm and whined. "If Molly could talk to us, she'd enlighten our world. Now I deliver this service to Josh. Amen."

Reverend Jacob moved over to the side of the sanctuary. Josh and Joyce walked behind the altar and faced the congregation.

Joyce spoke. "Each of us must finally meet the Great Silence alone on this circle of life. Children and the elderly are closest to our Creator. Bill Catches is touching the Great Spirit. His soul flowed through three mediums—the Ojibwa, the Catholic, the Signs Followers. Comfort was his in his last days. His wish was to be cremated and his ashes spread onto the river."

Silence.

The drumbeat of Billy Blackhawk resonated from the church to the hillsides, flowing down to the river valley. And the crowd rose as Billy appeared in the doorway, leading Father Joshua holding the black box with Joyce at his side, followed by Shanaya, her grandchildren, then Ted, Molly, and Oliver, with Sheriff Mad and Marshal McClelan in the rear. And all entered the line winding down to the river as the black box passed. The procession filled the riverbanks.

Father Joshua, holding the black box, stood on a hillock of the bank with Joyce. At one time he welcomed the sound of "Father." Now it remained a small part of him, but still a part. He wanted simply to be Josh. But it trailed him. Or at times did he trail it? The funeral procession filled the riverside upstream from their perch on that mound. Their ill-conceived plan was to sprinkle the ashes onto the water, allowing the gushing water to dissolve and absorb the remains of Bill Hatches. So all must be upstream; the water here, a mere three feet deep, made for easy access. Joyce had arranged for her grandmother to be carried on a bier by two of her students down the hill. She was escorted by two Native American Marine Corps sergeants carrying the flag.

Joshua and Joyce tracked down from their knoll, the crowd pushing in close. As Josh stepped into the river, Joyce at his side, a snake slithered under water against his boot, resurfaced downstream, and glided across. Reverend Jacob pointed as the serpent was wriggling along the other bank. "They fear us."

They hesitated momentarily and began to slosh through the river, Joyce holding onto his belt as he elevated the black box above his head. The bier with Shanaya accompanied by her military guards entered the river just behind Joyce and Joshua. After Shanaya's children and grandchildren, Ted, Oliver, and Molly made their way out but kept to the shallows, allowing Molly to breathe above water. Those who dared, tread the chilling water only in their cotton garments, moccasins, or boots. A few men, clad only in deerskin loincloths, made their way out with the crowd.

The crowd settled. Only the river's murmurings rose from the valley. Joyce nodded at the military guard.

"Bill is a Marine," said one of the guards. "And it is only right to be in water to commemorate his service and memory. No words can touch his life." They set the folded flag on the bier at the feet of Shanaya, who sat upright against a backrest.

"Thank you. And may the Great Spirit protect you," Shanaya said.

Joyce nodded to Josh. He opened the black box. "Water gives life," he said, and slowly poured Bill's ashes onto the river, while the tune from the flute of Billy Blackhawk drifted over the current and congregation.

Coop leaned against an oak on the opposite side of the river. He had settled there before sunrise to attend the funeral. In the long shadows of the setting sun, he stood and walked to the riverbank. The river and hillsides were empty, quiet. He sat down on a fallen oak and listened to the river.

RAPTURE RIVER

And his mind drifted with the river, his thoughts surfacing to those horrible moments when he had to play dead on that killing field as the enemy counted the dead before they moved on. He had lain on his stomach with his hands clutching his cross—the decapitated head of a fellow soldier at his side, severed arms and legs lying on his back, all his platoon dead. The enemy soldier counting bodies sped past this horror. Coop survived but the life remaining was a severed life, an existence without speech or hearing. The explosion stole his hearing and the flying legs, arms, and heads under which he lay his speech. He crawled out of this bloody grave and waded across a river that flowed red, eventually reaching a barn. He very seldom looked at the cross but felt it between his fingers. He was naked without it.

Gripping the cross in his pocket, he waded across the stream and trudged up the hill to the chapel. Outside the church he was led to the statue of St. Francis. He followed his nose as sweetgrass was thickly draped over the outstretched arms. He picked up some sweetgrass and hung it over the outstretched fingers. He felt a tap on his shoulder. He jerked around and stepped back.

Lewis raised his palm and said, "Peace."

Coop nodded.

Lewis took a gambling token out of his pocket. And Coop responded by raising his cross. Lewis ran his hand across his neck and then tapped his forehead. Coop stepped back and shook his head. Coop could not deal with death, no matter who.

They walked over to the statue of St. Kateri and knelt down by the turtles at her feet.

Chapter 24

As Josh drove down the hill to the Signs Followers Mission, the fog coiled around the abandoned schoolhouse. He parked immediately in front of the entrance and stepped out of his pickup. The mist curled up as the morning sun streamed over the field. The reverend was nowhere in sight. Josh opened the mission door and walked in. Reverend Jacob was prostrate in the middle aisle, lying on his stomach. He didn't move, unaware of Josh. Josh understood his state of meditation, so he sat down quietly in the rear. He'd meditate along with the reverend in the sacred stillness.

Yes, sacred stillness. The mind creates the sacred—no matter what that sacred appears to be. It's here. All one has to do is create it. He had driven Joyce to her sacred stillness at dawn. He parked at the foot of Rattlesnake Bluff and walked down the deer trail with her until she stood for a minute, and they hugged each other. "I'll see you in two days." She was departing on her vision quest with a day backpack, some food, very little, and a large canteen of water. She said that nature always entered her lone world and told her something.

By the time she was on the summit of Rattlesnake Bluff and observing her spirit world, he was in the Signs Followers Mission meditating with Reverend Jacob. Where was the connection for spiritual environment for this encounter? And the more he thought about it, the more he realized that her choice was. Could he compete with her emotional connection? He could see her now peering into the passing clouds, the sun penetrating her world and now his. Would there be snakes out this early? Probably not.

Joyce looked down upon the valley and gazed at the threshold of her vision quest. Nature would reveal herself alone—pure and simple. She'd wait to gather her thoughts, allow nature to soak into her mind—give up the other world. You wouldn't search for any answer to your question but allow nature to present answers. And then unmask the question that nature asked. If the spirit would allow an answer in search of a question. A riddle of the end in search of the beginning. She spread her blanket on the grass and stuck four sticks at four corners—earth, air, fire, and water or north, south, east, west. No matter. There was only above and below. Below, Mother Earth. Above, Father Sky. And she was below. Below what? Was the Great Spirit above and below, or just in her? Yes, in her. Her grandmother encouraged her to travel on her own path. "You do not need the exact ceremonies of your elders. They will come to you naturally, without learning or being taught." But her thoughts were messy. Messy as the deer trails meandering through the woods. Messy as the mayflies above the river in their motley display to prolong life. Messy as the feasting of the swallows rolling above to capture life to continue their own belonging to each other.

ROBERT EDWARD SMITH

The Great Spirit guides and doesn't guide. If she remained still and quiet, her mind would allow her to see through this messy world. The mess she was in now—a loving mess. Mess was the only word that came into her mind. And she saw the mess of the hawk swimming above as it glided orderly but unaware of its order. The mess of nature and of couples chasing each other and coupling. Of sitting on this hill as the day timed itself out. How could this mess be thought of, if it could be thought of at all—the mess of creation. But the mess was a timely mess as all human messes are. Is there order in nature? What echoes will my messy mind give to the clouds? Is that the tail of a jet over to the west? No way to escape this messy paradise of man's never-ending gall to leave his mark on the carpet above. And coax the unmade world to transform itself into the paradise you envisioned. And then the tail of the jet curled upon itself to twirl into a mirage that dove deep into the gray of her consciousness. And out of it as she strode fast into the vast depth of this image of the music of sadness that clung to her from her loss. And then the buzzing in her mind. Buzzing, buzzing, buzzing. And she kept from shouting. There was a time when she believed in Thunderbirds. Believed? No. Saw them. Not only in her dreams, where they appeared so often, but also when she was patiently lingering by the river with Drummer, her grandpa's dog, his fourth Drummer spaniel, and after a time the spirits of her ancestors emerged from the bubbling. And as she looked above, the large bird with a huge wingspan would appear and cool the river and her ancestors as they gathered.

But she could not get it out of her mind that these huge birds were only created by her mind. How did they get there? And why was she the only one of seven children to touch one? It actually ate a dead mouse out of her hand. When she told her grandmother, she said that it was wonderful. And she replied to her grandma that it wasn't an it but a she. And she hoped she would hold one of her chicks someday. And once, the bird flew over her with two of her offspring. And she watched them play, chasing each other above the trees. And she always went to bed with the hope that they would return to her dreams. And when they did, they welcomed her back into their zigzagging flight above the trees. She put out her hand, and a bee landed on her middle finger. And she looked into its compound eyes. How many does she see in me? "Hello," she said. "Good morning." And the bee nodded and buzzed. A meeting that she could not imagine. She never met a bee, and now all this time alone with a bee. Her vision would be with this bee over the next two days. Was that buzzing in her ears real or was it created from inside? What is real? How does the buzzing sound to the bees? And what do the bees think I am? Am I a bee? And if I am, could I just buzz on forever? Is it the smell of flowers that attracts me and clings to me as I flit from flower to flower? I flit off into the nothingness of the air. No. Am I but a space and cannot hide from my thoughts, which are nothing anyway? Am I the queen bee and what privilege does that give me? Bees simply are.

Her mind was entering the blank slate view, really no view, that allows the spirit to enter and heal her loss—the river of recovery had already started to flow through her.

Chapter 25

Ted was sitting at his fly-tying table, working on a Pale Evening Dunn. Not working, creating. Another night was being created as the moon crept above the horizon. His phone rang. "Molly, fetch me my phone. Sorry to wake you up."

She stretched, yawned, stood up on all fours, shook herself, and looked at Ted. Why can't I talk? I know what's going on and yet I'm kept in this never-ending, invisible muzzle. Unbearable at times. She moved over to the stump by the door, flipped the phone on its edge, and gently grabbed it with her teeth. I should just crush it in my bite. I don't like it any more than Ted. Why doesn't he throw it out? Toss it into the river. No, not that. Contaminate the river. Bury it, like a bone—a sacrilege, against our holy dog religion. I wish I could laugh. She placed the phone in Ted's open palm.

Ted petted her nose. "Thank you, Molly. A call from whom? I'm not in the mood to speak with the warden. If it's Lewis, I'd welcome it. But Lewis doesn't have or need a phone. Smoke signals are more reliable. So what if the wind is blowing in the wrong direction."

Molly's ears perked up. She tilted her head in that quizzical gesture that said, Well, what ya gonna do.

He leaned over and picked a black tick off Molly's ear. "I'm not going to answer it, and I worry more about these little bugs than what could be on that phone." He stood and shuffled over to the woodburning stove, opened the glass door, and flicked the tick in, then picked up a piece of kindling and placed it in the flames. And the fire kindled the nightmare of his teenage years in the aluminum extrusion plant. "Molly, it's your luck, no, good fortune that you didn't see the flames in the cast house and the screaming that sad night when three Black men burned to death. They said that the Blacks could stand the heat. I can see the molten aluminum flowing across the cement. I couldn't help them. That will always be with me till I pass."

Molly whined. She walked over to the door.

"You want out? So do I."

They walked up the hill toward Johnson's grave with Molly leading. "Someone is getting there before us, Molly. Our shadows. The moonlight and starlight make dark, our dark side."

When they reached the top of the hill, which was well lit, Ted sat on the boulder beside the gravestone with Johnson's plaque. *Molly squatted beside him and wondered if he would doze off.* She moved off to the side as Ted slid off the rock, balancing himself with his cane. *Come, Ted, come. Down, Ted, down. Commands she heard countless times. If she could only speak. She could make an excellent master. There you go, boy, not girl. Now slide your legs and rest your back against the rock and get some shut-eye.*

"If I doze off, Molly, wake me before the witching hour. You know, midnight."

Well, doze off and I'll have one of our meetings. Take forty winks. And as Ted drifted off, Owl hooted.

Molly looked up. Owl was perched on the limb of an oak tree. "Have you been there all this time spying on us?"

"I haven't been spying. I've been waiting for the door to our meeting to open. And now is our time together again. We have not had an evening meeting in a long time."

"Not everybody can come. Crow is roosting," said Molly.

"But we Nocturnals are all up," said Owl, "Whip-poor-will, Possum, Raccoon, Rat, Deer, Bobcat, and maybe Nighthawk. Nighthawk, she likes dusk and dawn best. And maybe some feral cats and, mind you, Snake and Turtle, and I almost forgot Bat."

And when Owl said Bat, Bat landed on the rock above Ted's head.

"And we could also invite Monarch Butterfly. Nighthawk will flit into the dark and round up our meeting," said Owl.

"Do I have anything to say in this matter?" said Nighthawk as she swayed on the limb of a maple tree directly above Bat. "Oh, excuse me, Bat, good evening."

"And good evening to you, Nighthawk," said Bat.

"Did I hear that right? A butterfly, a monarch?" said Nighthawk.

With a tremendous pounding of her wings, Owl crashed down onto the limb Nighthawk was perched on. "Does that answer your question?" Owl asked. "Or are more definitive *instructions required. Let me add this. They fly greater distances than you ever dreamed of. And under constant threats. We accept all living creatures. Or are you prejudiced?"*

"Of course, I'm prejudiced," said Nighthawk.

"I'm not prejudiced," said Whip-poor-will. "And I am a nightjar just like Nighthawk. We both are bug eaters. Now can't we forget our roles we play in our daily life and get into our dream time? Otherwise, we will never get along in this silly human world, and I mean silly."

"Wisely spoken," said Owl. And Owl thrashed her tremendous wings and rose above the hill suspended below the starlight, her shadow cast upon the congregation of living creatures assembling below. "If you scan the starlight above, you will see star groups man has called constellations that he has imagined as creatures with wings—birds. Assemble all you night creatures with wings, without wings."

And the hill was alive.

"Let us first of all hear from Turtle," said Owl.

"I ain't got much," said Turtle. "But I've got something mighty interesting. One day I was just a floating downstream when suddenly I flipped over and continued downstream, passing two fishermen. The few days before were also really odd when I saw an old Indian stumbling down the hill. Then he just disappeared into a gully."

"Well," said Nighthawk, "from my viewpoint above, I saw the whole thing. And what a thing. Molly, as she will tell, will relate the whole incident."

And Molly retold that afternoon on the river. "Nothing will escape us knowing what the river is, has done, or will do," concluded Molly. "Her power is more than all the stars and planets and suns and moons in the sky above us. But all the night above us is reflected on her waters, and she swal-

lows all into her depths and is master of all who touch her waters. No one can tell her whole story. All of us here will add to her story but not the whole story because only she knows her own course."

And the congregation of creatures stood in rapt attention, circling Molly as she stood next to Ted lying in the shadows.

"Even Snake here must know stories that will be news," said Molly.

"Oh my! Yes, I can," said Snake. "A funeral by the river I was at. And the bier was carried down from the hill of Saint Peter the Fisherman Mission. And the hills were just overflowing with humans. A snake up there didn't even have enough room to slither on. Well, we know how to take care of ourselves around humans because mostly they are afraid of us. By and by they reached the river with the bier. Now I was under a log sticking out over the river and when Lewis—y'all know Lewis." And the collected assembly chirped, barked, purred, growled, and squealed. "Y'all love Lewis as I do. When Lewis stepped on the log, I skimmed over the river and hid in the high grasses on the opposite bank. But the reverend serpent handler saw me, and he said he saw the devil." And the assembled congregation let out a roar of laughter.

"But no one, not even Monarch Butterfly saw what I saw," said Bobcat. "I roam the nights for my dinner. And you may be my supper, also supper for my two pups, but during our occasional meetings we suspend our appetites—or should I say surrender our hunger—and join to celebrate the river, or should I say our river. What I saw—I witnessed two murders on the river. I know and the river knows. But I respect the river's right to her secrets, which will only spill over as her time allows. She can't talk as we are privileged to by Ted in our gatherings, but our main interest is the *love story that bubbles up. How will our two lovers not be drowned in their silly human prejudices. And as Molly will relate how she saved Joyce from her own drowning, which I witnessed from a distance from my den. We are an instrument of the river, and what we do, we know not why we do it. Pray tell me if I am not right."*

Monarch Butterfly flew from the branch of a witch hazel tree. *"Excuse me, Bobcat, no, I didn't see what you saw. And thank you for respecting the river. But I'd like to digress for a few moments on your statement 'we know not why we do it.' I could never cope with the arduous flight and life that I'm given. But I accept what that is. And I cling to life. I fly all the way to Mexico. But I don't get there; the next generation gets there. I live to bear young. My life is short, but I celebrate every minute of it. I have little to contribute, but the hermit who lives in the deep forest is the human I have spent the most time with. I feel most comfortable with him. He was sitting on a stump. He looked at me with those deep, rheumy eyes. And of course I looked back, and we spent many days together. He communicated with me. He's a beautiful human. And if he could speak, he would teach humans much. But neither can we, no matter how much and profound are our insights into human behavior. We are locked into Ted's dreams. I know of no one here who realizes the opportunity we possess and how we could deliver our lovers from the wet weight of their mindless quarrels."*

Bat fluttered upon his branch. *"Don't worry, Monarch, we're harmless to each other. But there is one situation that I know I'm the only member of our esteemed group to witness. I was in the church hanging upside down from an overhead beam when our two lovers met in the church. And what a scene it was. I flew in on the sly when Father Josh let the* door fly open. See, now I'm being influenced by the ripples from Ted's dream waves. Everything is dominated by the river. I meant to say just Josh."

"It would be good to hear about their quarrels from the male viewpoint," said Molly.

"Even though I was not invited to your last meeting," Bat said, "I overheard Mrs. Rabbit's hilarious narrative of their intimate encounter in the river."

"Thank you," Rabbit let out. "I snuck in. And I feel I have not been invited. Rumors fly in these woods."

"So, what should we pay attention to—the two murders or the two lovers," said Rat.

"Why, of course, the two lovers," said Molly boldly.

"Continue please," said Owl firmly.

"Thank you, Owl," said Bat. "But let's get together on my abilities as an observer first. If you just point your ears up, you can hear a lot. That's why we bats have such big ears. Our chirping voices bounce off our surroundings and come back to our hearing, and we not only see but hear our way through the dark. That's why we are out and about at night. So with that click of the church key as the door opened, I entered before Josh. I always wondered why the Mission Church drew so many into its chambers. Chambers sounds like a horror story. Excuse me. Well, let me think. Spirit world? No, must be something better. Spirit haven. Not a heaven, but a haven. Haven, like a haven for wildlife, man and beast, where we respect each other. I was there when the funeral for the old Indian was celebrated. Snake was down by the river, but I hung in the rafters then. And Molly was there. She was not only there but conducted the ceremony. She couldn't talk, but the assembled haven felt her presence."

Molly barked. "Yes, I was, Bat, and with such anguish that I wish I could have given the eulogy by Reverend Jacob. But he did a fine job."

"That he did," said Bat. "But more about our two lovers. They met in that haven to give comfort to each other. The comfort that Molly gave to Joyce when she saved her on the river. When Joyce entered the church, there were three candles burning, and when she left there were only two. You know why she was taken apart when this happened, but no one gave Josh credit for being there with her and understanding the grief she suffered that day. And she told how Molly saved her from the river. And I saw the spirit entering both of them that evening."

And the congregation of animals clapped.

Bat continued: "We are spirits, one and all here, celebrating and rejoicing an animal life, the only life we know. The humans are mere spirits also, as we are, but they celebrate and rejoice their human life. Why are we so alike in raising our young? We never learned hate as the humans. We learned conflict and aggression but not hate. The one element of our learning which we use to our advantage. Humans overanalyze love, and we just give in to it. And why do the Native Americans go on a vision quest in the hope that they will cross paths with an animal who will guide them in their life, who may even speak to them and encourage their growth by deepening their spirit?

"A spirit chamber is where I was. A spirit castle," said Bat. "Our whole forest is our castle. Mine might be a cave in our forest but not something artificial as a mere building in which their great spirit thrives. We thrive everywhere in our castle, a castle without walls. And we don't need a castle keeper as Josh so humbly claimed to be. Our mere presence in the forest is a reason for celebration. So, suffer these children, humans."

Rat stood up on all fours and scampered to the center of the animal circle that ringed Ted. "I've got something that I'm feeling," Rat said. "I know I'm getting smarter by the minute, by the light of the moon, maybe."

Owl flapped her wings and dropped down from her perch, and Rat scurried off to the side.

"Sorry to frighten you so," said Owl. "But I know we all are."

"Let's listen to her wisdom before the night steals us away," said Raccoon. "I should know. Humans say I look like a bandit with the black fur around my eyes. And there I go talking like a human."

"That doesn't surprise me," said Owl. "We are riding on the waves of Ted's dreams. There is a word—archetype—that comes into play here. We were here way before any humans were here. As they came into being, they all evolved from what came before. Some of our thoughts and some of our beings are in them. They are not as fortunate as some of us are like us birds. They can't fly, but they think too much, and their dreams allow us to enter their world. They become more like us, and we become more like them. We ride on their dreams, and they ride on our natural world. And Ted here, because he knows what is important in his life, lives as close to a natural life as can be had. Thanks to Molly."

"I appreciate your gratitude," said Molly, "and there will be a time when we are all united and share in the comfort of each other's closeness. But what has brought us together is this love and this hate. The love between the Native American and the fallen priest. And the hate that burns inside the killer. Can we make this killing stop or are we predestined to endure this forever?"

"We all are getting smarter by the minute as we live off and communicate with Ted's brain waves," said Owl. "Does everyone here feel like they're getting smarter?"

The circle became alive with barks, twitters, meows, and howls.

"That's what I thought," said Owl. "We think and talk better as we dive deeper into Ted's brain vibrations. And one human named Jung said that we are knocking on the door of hidden dreams. I heard Reverend Jacob say that."

"Look up," said Snake.

"A falling star," shouted Bat.

"An omen," said Bobcat. "My tail is short so I don't have to gain balance if I'm up high. But that star has a long tail of light behind it. It's guiding itself. What does it mean?"

"It means," said Owl, "that we can only observe and watch the river. Two lovers wander the woods and look up at the same falling star as we do. And question what their future is."

"They think too deep," said Gopher. "I'm underground most of the day, but I allow myself to come up at least once in a while to feel the earth."

"You're always welcome," said Owl.

"And," Gopher continued, "since I've been above with all of you, I love riding on Ted's waves. He must have the world floating around those lobes of his. And I feel like I'm getting smarter by the minute."

"Me too," said Bat, hanging upside down. "But oh, oh, Ted is stirring."

"Maybe he's having a bad dream," said Nighthawk.

"And the bad dream is us," said Rat.

"The bad dream ain't us," said Butterfly. "It's them, the humans."

"ZZZZZZZZZZ"

"Who dat," said Rat.

"It's me," said Queen Bee.

"What you doing here?" said Rat.

"What you, a rat, doing here? We pollinate the flowers so their life continues."

"Now, now," said Owl. *"Let us be civil. All of us belong here. Listen to Queen Bee. We welcome her insight."*

"Ted's dreams flow with the spirit of the river. We are sailing on his dreams as they surface from the ebb tides that have washed out and now resurge from far distant times when we were emerging."

"I'm getting smarter," said Rat. *"We are part of the evolution of life. How do I know that? I'm getting smarter by the minute."*

"Why do humans search us out in their vision quests?" said Bee. *"What could we tell them that they don't already know?"*

"How do I know?" said Rat.

"I was alone with Joyce on Rattlesnake Bluff," said Bee. *"And in her vision quest, I was the medium that she entered to journey in her vision quest. Her feet were grounded on that hill in the solid earth, but my life force carried her beyond into the spirit world. She read all the books in her schooling, but she doesn't know the top of Rattlesnake Bluff. She went up there for answers, without any questions. And we met without an appointment. And together we let it happen. With my buzzing and her thoughts. Her vision. And this hill was her library and her church. Her university. So, she believes in being with her thoughts on a high hill. And we crossed paths up there. We didn't have an appointment. The spirit of the hill let it happen. We make love and honey, buzzing*

around the lilacs. The great spirit is everywhere. And why do we have to go high up? The great spirit is everywhere, even in the ground under."

"Yes, he is," said Badger. *"And he is down under fighting for us. And what did she learn from you, if anything? Probably nothing. It could only bring up what is already lying there. And make her realize what she already knows. Which is a lot more than I know. If she's lucky she found out what she already knows."*

"We don't have all the answers," said Owl.

"Neither does Ted," said Molly. And the hill silenced as Ted yawned and stretched.

Molly moved to Ted and licked his fingers. The real world again.

Chapter 26

Molly sat on the bank under a cedar tree. The aroma always calmed her, and bugs and ants were scarce around cedars. She was watching her master, Ted, enjoy his early evening fishing. Ted cast his fly against a log jutting out from the bank. As he completed his cast, his rod flew out of his grasp. He clutched his chest and stumbled face down into the river. Molly plunged into the water, swam to his side, braced her hind paws against the gravel, clenched her teeth around the collar of his wool shirt, and strained to lift his face above water. She struggled to drag him onto the shallows. Halfway up the bank with his feet still dangling in the river, she rolled him over so that he was face up with his head resting on a dry clump of river grass. He tried to talk but couldn't. His eyes closed. Molly put her nose next to his mouth and felt his hot breath.

"Run, Molly, run," cackled Crow. "He's still with us. I'm riding on his waves. And everyone will congregate as I have in an instant."

The sky overhead turned black. Black from the flock of crows that had amassed there.

RAPTURE RIVER

Owl alighted on a cedar tree above Molly. "You'll have to run faster than you ever have to get our two lovers. Our only hope to save Ted. A Cooper's hawk will lead you through the swamp and pine forest on the shortest route. She can dodge trees and fly low. No better pilot. The flock of crows will be above, but the late afternoon sun will shine through. Molly, may the Great Spirit be with you."

Molly had no instant reply, only to act. All of her eighty-five pounds of muscle and instinct welled up inside her. And she ran as she had never run before.

Cooper's Hawk appeared above her. "You'll have to dive into the river to get to the other side to avoid the briar patches."

Molly plunged into the river and followed the hawk as she flew straight up the river and cut across to the opposite side.

And she was on a well-used deer trail through tall river grass below a hillside of scrub oak. And she wondered why she was born not to fly. Such a strange world with humans, birds, fish. She attempted to jump a steep gully but missed and tumbled into a muddy brush pile at the bottom. She felt imprisoned and looked up at Cooper's Hawk.

"Help is on the way," said Cooper's Hawk.

Beaver appeared at the edge and guided Molly to the logjam at riverside where Molly could escape, muddy but safe. Panting heavily, Molly pawed her way up the steep bank. She sensed she was nearing home. When she reached the top, she stopped. Not to rest but to trot carefully because she was near the spot, the death spot, where a black Labrador was found dead from a rattlesnake bite. She heard a rattle, or did her mind hear a rattle? Cooper's Hawk remained above as if suspended in midair. Cooper's Hawk heard the rattle. She perceived Eagle in flight. Eagle could not hear as well as she, nor smell as well as Molly, but she could see and see she did. The rattlesnake, wound up like a thick coil, its red tongue flickering in and out, was set to strike from its perch on a pine stump.

Molly froze, her front paw raised for her next step. They stared each other down, testing, teasing, challenging. The only sound was the rush of wind in the trees above as the eagle arrowed down and struck, its sharp claws piercing the snake between its eyes. Eagle pounded its wings and lifted the snake above the canopy, the snake dangling like a lifeless rope swinging from side to side.

Molly looked up at Cooper's Hawk. "Thank you."

"My pleasure, Molly," replied the hawk. "Eagle's meal for her hatchlings."

As she neared the site where she had found the woodchuck, she looked above at the black flock of crows that had shut out the daylight. Joyce was on the porch with Josh, and both stood up alarmed by the dark as if a shade had been pulled down over the sky.

Molly barked.

"Molly's here," Joyce said. "Where's Ted? Something's wrong." She ran down the two-track to the road. "Josh, bring some water. She's panting heavily... Molly, where have you been? You're all black and muddy and burry. Lie down, girl," and she knelt beside her and began picking out the twigs, burrs, and brush that clung to her blackened coat.

Josh placed a bucket of water at her side. Molly stood up and drank.

After drinking half the water, Molly walked toward the road.

She looked at Josh. "Had enough?" he asked.

"She wants us to go with her to find Ted. She had to run through the swamp to get here. Maybe he's injured—broke a leg or sprained an ankle. Or... Oh, Great Spirit, no," Joyce said.

"Go get your keys and give them to me. Ted is probably parked at McKinnan's Bend. Molly will lead us to him when we get there. Molly can ride in the bed. Why is that sky so dark?"

"You're driving?"

"Ted may be hurt. Oh...no. No. Gitchi Manitou. Great Spirit. Hope it's not serious."

Josh lowered the bed door and Molly jumped in. "I hope we make it there alive, Molly, what with that race car lady driving us. Hold on and don't fall out. She'll be taking some of these curves at ninety."

"You took that last intersection at sixty-five. Everyone stops there even without a stop sign on these dirt roads. Molly had to run all this way through the swamp. Lucky she didn't get bit by a rattlesnake."

"Molly is woods smart," Joyce said.

"You're woods smart. But…we're not on the Indianapolis racetrack."

"I'm afraid, Josh. I'm afraid. I know Molly. We understand each other. Ted may be in some serious danger."

"Okay. Gun it."

Joyce spotted Ted's Jeep and stopped. Ted had parked his Jeep on his well-worn off-road spot, a block from McKinnan's Bend. Molly had already jumped out of the bed and was paused on the deer path before Joyce and Josh stepped onto the ground from the pickup. They followed her.

When she reached the river, Molly stopped for them to catch up. They saw Ted across the river lying on the bank with his feet spread out into the shallows. She plunged into the river, and Joyce and Josh followed. Molly rushed to Ted's side and pressed her ear against his chest. *She heard weak beating. She sniffed at his mouth and sensed no breath.* Josh and Joyce knelt on either side of his chest. Ted slowly opened his eyes, but they shut suddenly. Josh placed two fingers on his neck—something, maybe nothing. Josh began artificial resuscitation by placing the heel of his coupled hands on his breastbone. He thrust downward and counted rhythmically with each compression.

Molly growled, leaped at Josh, and sunk her teeth into Josh's wrist.

"Molly, no," Joyce yelled.

Josh shook his wrist. "She drew blood. Why?"

"I'll tell you why," a voice sounded from the shadows. Lewis appeared on the bank along with Coop peering over his shoulder.

"Don't," Lewis said to Josh. "Stop. Molly understands, knows. She's better than any shaman. She knows Ted's soul is departing. No life can be poured back into him or forced back into him."

Molly looked up at Lewis, her tail wagging.

"He's departing to the land of the Great Spirit. He had a joyous life."

Coop nodded and took his hat off. A butterfly flew off his hat and alighted on the dry grass supporting Ted's head.

Coop smiled and tried to say something but couldn't.

"He can talk," Lewis said. "I heard him when he's alone in the woods. Butterflies congregate and form a halo around him. And I've heard him talking."

"Allow his spirit to depart," Joyce said. "And look up. The black mass of crows is breaking up, and the light is coming through. They sense his spirit rising but also remaining. There's always that struggle between the here and the now and the hereafter."

"Molly will sense that he is not and that his soul has departed," Lewis said.

The butterfly that had alighted on the dry river grass flew up and landed on Coop's hat. Coop gently took off his hat. The butterfly balanced for a few seconds and then hovered over the assembly of five and suddenly descended on Molly's nose. The overhead flock of crows dispersed. Molly shook her nose, and the butterfly flew off to the surrounding foliage.

"Do you feel any pulse?" Lewis said.

Josh knelt and felt for his jugular pulse. "Nothing."

"The river will part, open up, to welcome his soul on his final journey," Lewis said. "We best leave him here through the night to complete his crossing. Coop and I will remain with him till sunrise. Sheriff Mad can remove him tomorrow morning."

"He wished to be cremated and his ashes placed on the hill near Johnson's grave," Joyce said.

"We will greet Sheriff Mad at sunrise," repeated Lewis.

Joyce knelt and hugged Molly. "Can Molly stay the night? She was his spirit guide. And no one knows the river like Molly and Ted." Molly nuzzled her nose against her cheek.

Josh knelt beside them. All were silent until Owl hooted. And Molly wondered if this was announcing their last meeting. Joyce and Josh stood, splashed through the river, and departed.

Lewis and Coop sat on a pine stump. *Next to Coop, Monarch Butterfly alighted on the whorled leaf of a milkweed bush.* "His spirit is struggling," said Monarch. "His vibrations and the river's are one."

But only Owl could hear Monarch. And Owl replied, "Butterfly, your time has come to perform your magic. Cast your spell of sleep on Lewis and Coop. Sometimes I feel that Coop could be with us but not now. Such a beautiful person. And we will have our meeting of all the forest creatures. Now, perform your magic."

And Monarch alighted on the leaf of a milkweed plant. She unfolded her proboscis, a tiny, flexible, straw-like mouth, and sucked up white sap. She then hovered over Coop and Lewis and deposited a drop on their foreheads. Both fell into deep sleep.

"Now is the time for our gathering, our last meeting with Ted as our host. We are at the time of sunset, so all the forest life will be here," said Owl.

And they gathered from throughout the Black River Valley. All living, non-human creatures, to celebrate Ted's departure.

RAPTURE RIVER

"I'm here," said Molly.

"We understand your sorrow and mourning, but what would Ted expect. Yes, mourning but also celebration into the world of the Great Spirit. Gitchi Manitou."

And the riverside became more alive than it had ever been. Alive with birds, bobcats, skunks, otters, deer, porcupines, groundhogs, beavers, woodchucks, turtles, snakes, frogs, ducks, rabbits, bats, and brook trout schooling in the river, the river riling up and foaming as if a severe thunderstorm had hit.

And off to the side with her three cubs was Bear, the three cubs hugging around her and lifting their ears to see the party that had been called together.

"We will only have this last night together with Ted's waves and Molly's electricity," said Owl. "But will our world end now? Is this our last night together? I feel a certain weakness stealing into my thoughts. They are not as strong as usual."

"I'm a simple, lowly rat," said Rat, "but I have been given time, by the way, equal time, with Owl and Crow and Bobcat and even Bear. And look how we congregate and enjoy our time together. And all of us join in and are treated as equals."

"But," said Partridge, "our lives will be the same. Time passes and time also passes for our two lovers. Ted will not be here to guide them. And we certainly won't. And no one can foretell the future of our two lovers, not even the river. But there is one hope—Ted's spirit may hover over this valley, and we may, with the assistance of Molly, join together again."

"There will be no substitute for Ted," said Owl. "And the time for us to remain together while Ted's spirit hovers over this valley and becomes one with the river is now."

At midnight, on his cell phone, Sheriff Mad talked with Josh about the death of Ted. He walked outside and looked up at the full moon.

Lewis and Coop and Molly would stay with Ted through the night. And when the sheriff asked Josh if Ted was surely dead, Josh couldn't answer. And he related the whole story of attempting to resuscitate Ted and Molly stopping him—biting his hand and drawing blood. And Lewis and Coop appearing out of the night and commanding him as firmly as Molly to stop compressions. At sunrise he'd drive out there along with an ambulance, but with its siren off just in case there was a miracle. And lately he was beginning to believe in miracles.

This whole county has been flipped upside down. Ever since that snake charmer appeared and the murder along the river and the oil companies closing in on the investigation. And now the rumor spread by Lewis about Coop and the butterflies he talks to. And then the funeral of Bill Catches. He passed away just like Ted by the river, if not in it. So now we have two natural deaths and two murders. Why all these deaths along the river? And he was in the middle of it.

Sheriff Mad drove his patrol car out of the Elk County police station followed by an ambulance with the siren silenced. The fifteen-mile drive on this calm Sunday morning was not his usual morning foray into the wilderness. Driving north out of the morning sun's glare, he was on his way to pick up and deliver his best friend's body to the morgue. And he began to reminisce through the years that he and Ted had enjoyed. The sheriff wasn't the fisherman

RAPTURE RIVER

Ted was, but he enjoyed duck hunting with Molly. And Molly had run through miles of swamp to get to Josh and Joyce with the hope of saving Ted. But she was just a dog. No, he couldn't say that. She cared for all the time she had with Ted, and she knew what death was. He had phoned Josh that he was on his way, and Josh said he'd meet him when he got there.

As Sheriff Mad drove around a curve, Josh and Joyce were standing by the side of the road. Molly, probably with Ted.

He slowed to a crawl and stopped, the ambulance immediately behind him.

"No need to hurry," Josh said to the ambulance driver and his assistant. "Ted is gone." Earlier he had walked to the river and yelled across to Lewis, who said that Ted was gone. The river, riled up and foamy, had risen overnight, carrying down branches and twigs that she latched onto along the banks.

The ambulance attendants removed the folded stretcher with a body bag from the trunk.

Molly greeted Joyce and Josh. She trotted past them to the sheriff. He knelt and Molly nuzzled her nose against his neck. "So sorry, girl." A tear rolled down his cheek.

Molly then sniffed at the ambulance attendants who were unfolding the stretcher with the body bag.

"No body bag, boys," the sheriff said. "Respect for Molly. She knows Ted has passed. When you get back to the ambulance, you can do that. Maybe when you're down the road and out of sight."

"Yes, sir. We understand."

When they reached the river, Lewis yelled from the other side, "Go right in. The water will wake you up."

"Thanks, Lewis," Sheriff Mad said. "Can't you deliver to this side?"

"No such luck," replied Lewis. "Molly won't approve. And you can warm up by my fire. Both Coop and I overslept. The spirit world was active in the night and entered our dreamworld. Both Coop and I woke up alive but cold."

Molly stepped down the bank and stood at the river's edge. She barked and Joyce followed her across. Molly veered off upstream to avoid the deeper pools so she could cross without swimming. She stopped at Ted's corpse with his waders on and feet splayed out into the shallows.

Josh said, "We're next."

"With our boots on," the ambulance driver said.

"And pants. How else? Let's go." Josh led Sheriff Mad and the ambulance attendants across, following Molly's water trail.

"Do we get extra pay for this?" the ambulance driver asked.

"Only if you fall in," Sheriff Mad said. "Watch out for this rock. I almost stumbled on it."

When the sheriff reached the bank, Lewis waded into the water and gave him a hand. "Welcome, Sheriff Mad."

"Thank you, Lewis. An unusual funeral parlor."

"Yes, it is, but Ted would love this."

On the bank, the sheriff, Joyce, Josh, and the two attendants knelt around Ted. Lewis and Coop had to pull Ted farther up the bank during the night when the river rose, and they knelt around the clump of earth supporting Ted's head.

"Who closed his eyes?" one of the attendants asked.

Coop nodded.

A long silence. Until the sheriff looked at Joyce and Molly at her side and said, "We need a prayer, Joyce."

"I hear Ted talking to us slowly and deliberately with ease through this prayer."

RAPTURE RIVER

I give you this one thought to keep—
I am with you still, and do not weep,
I am a thousand winds that blow,
I am the diamond glints on snow,
I am the sunlight on ripened grain,
I am the gentle autumn rain.
When you awaken in the morning hush,
I am the swift, uplifting rush
Of quiet birds in circled flight.
I am the soft stars that shine at night,
Do not think of me as gone
I am with you still—in each cold new dawn.[3]

"Cold new dawn. And he is with us still," Lewis said.

"Amen," said Josh.

The two ambulance attendants began their duty while everyone retreated to the side. They loaded him onto the stretcher, handling his body as if he were still alive.

The funeral procession began, and everyone crossed the river, except Lewis and Coop. Now it was Ted's turn. As the ambulance attendants reached the middle of the river with the stretcher, the current spiked and the water level rose over two feet in seconds, splashing against the stretcher and nearly overturning it as Ted's arm dangled over the side into swirling rapids.

"The water is over my waist. I can hardly hold on," the front attendant said.

"We should have strapped him down," the other said. "At my end I'm having trouble just keeping his feet on."

Lewis yelled over the roar of rapids, "Just keep coming. The river wants Ted. She wants him."

---

[3] Native American Prayer for the Grieving," author unknown, churchgists.com. A revised version of the original poem "Do Not Stand by My Grave and Weep" by Mary Elizabeth Frye, which was written in 1932 and never published. The author intended it for the public domain.

Molly, already across at Joyce's side, barked and was amazed how rigid the earth—land and water—had grasped and held onto Ted's spirit. If she could only talk. Joyce could offer up a prayer. And with her bark Joyce started chanting, and the river listened:

> *I have only one chant now,*
> *One prayer.*
> *Gitchi Manitou, calm these waters*
> *And allow Ted's spirit to depart.*
> *He is gone now*
> *And only a few steps from having his physical*
> *Body vanish by the art of cremation, his desire.*
> *But the smoke and ashes that will remain*
> *Are of nothing*
> *Because his soul and spirit will always*
> *Drift with the river in this spirit world that*
> *Lasts forever.*
> *He'll possess these waters.*
> *So allow the river to rest.*
> *His life has been made holy*
> *With your waters.*

And the river swallowed its waters and calmed. The ambulance attendants in the middle of the river were stunned by the sudden change—the river level decreased by two feet, and the rapids were no more. The river flowed without anger in a few seconds.

"The spirit of the river has answered Joyce's prayer," Lewis said.

The stretcher was laid down when they reached the bank, and both attendants sat next to each other, welcoming the solid earth—Mother Earth. On the other side Lewis and Coop had vanished into the swamp.

"You boys need rest," Sheriff Mad said. "Now do you believe in

RAPTURE RIVER

miracles as I do?"

Both answered in unison, "Yes, sir." Molly sat on her haunches between them with their arms around her. "An unusual dog," the driver said, "almost human."

Sheriff Mad looked up. "I don't see any flying rabbits…yet… Maybe tomorrow."

When they reached the road, they set the stretcher down behind the ambulance, opened the trunk, and rolled the body bag off to the side. Molly watched as they slid the stretcher onto the rack.

"You boys wouldn't object if Molly rode along in the back next to Ted," the sheriff said.

"No, sir, absolutely not."

"She needs to say a long goodbye."

The ambulance drove into the Elk County Funeral Home parking lot with Molly in the back next to Ted. Joyce and Josh followed in his small pickup. The ambulance stopped. The attendants opened the trunk, and Molly leaped down, sat off to the side, watching them remove the stretcher. Josh parked alongside. When Joyce opened her door, Molly sprang to her side. Joyce knelt and they hugged each other.

Molly whined.

"There are no words I can say that will make it any easier for you, Molly. Let's hug each other."

But Molly had deep concerns. Joyce doesn't know how I'm able to ride on Ted's brain waves along with the other forest non-humans. What do I call them? And what am I, a creature? But now I have a new master and mistress. And she watched as the body was delivered through the back door into the funeral parlor with Josh along its side.

"No body bag," the mortician said.

"None. Molly's request," Josh said.

"Who's Molly?"

"Ted's dog. Or should I say golden Lab. She knows more about Ted and us than most humans know about each other. But Ted requested cremation and, I believe, he had that set up with you."

"Yes, he has. Didn't want any fancy urn. Just a black cardboard box. We'll have that for you in a week. Know what's the future of his ashes?"

"Yes," Josh said.

"Any visitation?"

"No."

"I'll call the *Elk Herald,* and it'll be in the obituary column tomorrow. Who's the executor of his will?"

"I am," Josh said. "He has four daughters. I'm sure they'll attend. We'll have an outdoor memorial ceremony by the river. Ted's wishes."

"Sometimes that's best," the mortician said. "What with the family quarrels that at times emerge. What about his cabin and Molly."

"He's left the cabin to me and, of course, Molly. Joyce will care for her. His four daughters are married, and well-off."

Chapter 27

Josh and Joyce drove from Elk Village down the gravel road with Molly in the truck bed to his cabin, not Ted's cabin anymore, never. Never. Never. Never. "Ted's not there forever," Josh said, "forever more." The last twenty-four hours had been exhausting. Joyce had heard nothing he'd said. She had disappeared into one of her trances with her palm held against the road wind as if begging for peace. He stopped on the two-track to Ted's cabin. Joyce relaxed her hand and said, "We're here. You and me and Molly."

Both stepped out of the truck. "Where's Molly?" she said. Molly, seldom, if ever, slept in the bed of the truck, but this morning was an exception. Joyce lowered the back gate. Molly stood, stretched, and jumped down. "We all need a bath. Let's go into Ted's, no, our shed and give you a bath after I pick all those burrs and twigs out of your beautiful golden coat."

Joyce sat down on the stump Ted usually sat on to prepare pelts for fly tying. Molly reluctantly came to her side.

Molly sniffed around the stump and sat down in front of Joyce. *She looked up at Joyce as if she were going to have a nice womanly, casual conversation.*

"Well, what do you have to say, Molly?"

ROBERT EDWARD SMITH

Molly looked at her and began to walk around the stump in ever-increasing circles. She stopped when she was about a dozen feet away and stared at Joyce, hesitated a few minutes, and then began to circle back around until Joyce could touch her. And she began to whine. And she wondered if she would ever be able to survive without Ted. And now their meeting with the animal world could cease. Would there now be nothing? Who could replace Ted? Josh. Joyce. Maybe Coop. She could see Josh and her moving closer together now. But how close. Josh and Molly moving closer together. But would that interfere with Joyce and Josh and their closeness. And she sensed that the change was not just the physical attraction alone. She sensed this from their auras. Their energy fields meshed with one another. They were melting into one circle. And she wondered. Is this the beginning of what humans call love?

She looked up into Joyce's eyes, and Joyce looked down into hers. Joyce said, "I'm just like you, Molly. We're more alike than different. You were here before me as a species. We think like you. We have the same emotions, but we call ourselves human and you're called animal. If we could only see this and if everyone could see it, we would have a better world. Since I'm Native American I am closer to the animal world than maybe Josh. But Josh is growing and developing into his more natural self. He is a good man. He just doesn't trust his instincts."

RAPTURE RIVER

And Molly was aware that she was thinking out of the box— the little box of her doghood. But Ted's passing on had not sunk into her womanhood, her girlhood. She was aware that her heightened thinking abilities were carrying her beyond—to where she didn't know. Was Ted still there guiding her to that netherworld between two worlds? Would she be able to bounce back to those long moments of joy? The complete removal of Ted from this world was not now. And she hoped it would never be. All this wilderness life would thrive with or without Ted.

"Let's clean you up," Joyce said. "The first time I talked to Ted, he was casting flies on Little Dipper Lake. And that was before you were born. I was just beginning my teaching job at the Peace Gathering. That was a time of my trials. I needed the wilderness just as you do, Molly. That was a transition time for me. And now this is a major transition time for you, Molly. Josh will also have difficulty with this new life without Ted, but you will survive. How do you like your new master, Josh, and your new mistress, me?"

Inside the cabin Josh sat at Ted's fly-tying table and wondered if he should attempt to complete Ted's last unfinished fly that he had probably left before going with Molly on his last day on the river. He had told Josh that if he didn't return with any fish, he'd always have something to look forward to. Josh never would equal his art. Josh glanced at the photo on the end of the table with his wife and four daughters. Ted had strong memories that carried him through his many years. But the last ten years were also kept exciting with his companionship. Then there was Joyce. He stood up from the table and walked over to the side window. Joyce loved Molly. And Molly was healing and uniting them.

ROBERT EDWARD SMITH

When Joyce finished removing all the burrs and thorn twigs, she opened the shed door, and Molly followed her to the utility tub. She moved a three-step stair in front of the tub, and Molly willingly walked up and climbed in. She attached the hose to the faucet and began spraying Molly from head to paw. *How welcome to get rid of all that muck from the swamp was Molly's only thought.*

But Molly felt something she did not know what to call. It was a new sensation about her world. A new feeling about the space she lived in. She was fresh and clean in her outside world after Joyce's scrubbing and the drying of her golden coat with Joyce's hair dryer. But she noticed that her thinking was not drowned out. It was like she was under water, and she was born onto a new earth. She didn't know what to call it or name it. But it, whatever it was, was new. And she saw herself as new. Could it be Ted's spirit melting into her because it didn't have any place to go? Her thoughts were becoming more human thoughts than animal thoughts. Was Ted alive in her? She had only felt this way when Ted was napping in the valley. She flew on his brain waves. He isn't asleep; he's gone now. Not all gone. This valley won't allow him to go, not holding him as a prisoner but allowing his spirit to choose its final resting place, in the freedom of this valley forever.

Chapter 28

As the sun was setting on the first day of their newly acquired home, Molly, Joyce, and Josh were sitting at the table overlooking the river.

They had plans to make. There would be no formal funeral. All four daughters had been contacted by Josh during a very long day. They had planned a ceremony on the hill adjacent to Johnson's grave. Ted's ashes would be scattered over the earth, and Josh would offer prayers for his spirit. Sheriff Mad, Lewis, and Coop would be in attendance. Sheriff Mad would also invite Marshal McClelan and Reverend Jacob without his snakes.

And Molly wondered if the power of Ted's spiritual presence would allow her to call together another meeting.

Molly, with her soft manners, was sitting at the table on the third chair, Ted's chair, when Josh addressed Joyce. "I didn't know you had psychic powers. Spiritual, heavenly powers, to still the waters. You commanded the river, and it obeyed." *And Molly saw Joyce with that facial expression she had encountered before and knew that it was best if she retired to her bed under Ted's fly-tying table. Something of Ted's. Could she, would she ever allow his presence to rest? Escape she would into her own dreamworld.*

"Mother Earth and Father Sky," Joyce said, "allowed the river to become a bridge between the then and now. The now of Ted's spirit passing. But a bridge does not only go one way. It is a two-way path that will allow Ted to return to his home. All shamans throughout the world as far away as Russia recognize Mother Earth and Father Sky. Was it a miracle that I performed?"

"That's what the sheriff said at the funeral home," Josh said.

"Well, just as well that he believes in magic. This world needs more magic." Joyce glanced at Molly under the fly-tying table and then stared out the window at the river below. "The river winds, doesn't she, just to get this far. So many bends and banks that she nourishes and comforts. But could this have been a natural disaster?"

"A natural disaster. Like what?"

"What if a dam broke? A beaver dam on Rattlesnake Creek or Hardwood Creek? There are beaver dams on both those tributaries. The Black is the main throughway of this entire valley. If they broke upstream, a sudden rush could cause the river to swell and the current gush and, as we witnessed, almost carry Ted away on his stretcher. Did this twist of fortune pull off what we call a miracle? In my last vision quest on Rattlesnake Bluff, I waited and waited and waited for something to come my way to deliver a truth, an insight. It didn't work. So, I sat and enjoyed my night and day universe—sun, moon, stars, wind. In other words, Mother Earth. And when I least expected it, a bee alighted on a flower, a lupine. And that's when I commenced looking at my surroundings and losing myself and becoming one with Mother Earth. Did Mother Earth see me then and allow me to be one with my environment? I don't know. But I became hypnotized by that bee. And my soul, whatever you want to call it, conjoined with the earth. I had only myself, the Great Spirit, and Mother Earth. Coop is now getting in touch with himself. And it's taking a monarch butterfly."

"Coop, yes, another miracle," Josh said. "But then there's Molly."

"Molly. Who does she belong to now? When she ran through

the swamp and trotted up the two-track, she came to me first. No reflection on you, Josh. She loves us equally, but she came to me first when in need. I was present when she delivered. And she was with me when I miscarried. Some bonding went on then. But I feel that she is becoming more human—or are we becoming more dog savvy?"

"Probably both," Josh said.

"Show me your wrist where she bit you… Look at that. And that was last evening. I can make out her teeth marks. That's what I mean absolutely—her humanness. She knew Ted was about to go, so she stopped you from interfering with his passing over into the Happy Hunting Grounds or Fishing Grounds. Did you see the halo around Ted when they were carrying his bier across the river?"

"I saw some brightness around the ambulance attendants. It was like a halo underwater encircling Ted. Did you create that too?"

"Nothing was created. The spirit of Ted held the river, and the river knew it. And probably only because Molly was there. Molly is uniting us to that river more than we know. The only thing she can't do is talk. We are animal. We evolved from the animals that preceded us. We have an animal nature just like Molly. We evolved from monkeys and dogs before that. Molly is showing us the way back into our animal. We were animals before we were human. We know it but don't care to think about it because we feel we are far superior to any animal. But are we? Not in our sense of smell, not in our sense of the earth's magnetism that birds and insects are aware of. We landed on the moon before we understood the migratory pattern of the monarch butterfly. Something as simple as a butterfly flying. More complicated than a space rocket. What if robots are created that will replace our dogs, first, and then us? Some scientists believe we don't need our bodies anymore. All our bodies do is get sick, get in our way. But we're stuck with what we've got. I'm not trying to say that we should become like animals but that we should appreciate our animal nature. And realize just how close we are to our dogs. We are 99 percent monkey. So, are we more like them or are they more like us?"

"I hope they are more like us. But then we can't deny our animal nature."

"That's why Native Americans adopt animals as their spirit guide. But I am not a red-tailed hawk."

"I haven't taken an animal identity. But if I did it would probably be a brook trout."

"Good choice, considering all you could choose from.

"If human lives matter, no matter what color, creed, or gender then all humans matter, then all animals matter because humans are animals. Then you may ask about hunting. We thank the Great Spirit for the gift of the animal who has met death at our hands. But look at us, Josh. You, Josh, had animal magnetism. Now, don't look away and be embarrassed by your…well, let's say attractiveness, for lack of a better term. Look at the procreative parts of us and how we were attracted to each other. Our animal ruling our emotions and behavior. And we created together the tiny heart that once beat in me. We procreate in the same identical manner in which the animals of all species continue their existence—physically."

Molly glanced up from her bed. Why don't you just go to sleep? I've had a long day.

"It appears that Molly wants to talk. Maybe she needs a companion—a cat?"

"A cat… What next," Josh said.

"Lewis has a cat that just had a litter—four little kittens. A few weeks old now and I fell in love with one of the kittens, a female. It's a breed of cat called Maine coon. She has a fluffy coat and is chocolate brown with white paws and a white streak on her nose. They're known as the gentle giants of the cat world, and they get quite large—fifteen to twenty pounds. You should hear how they mew at each other. Molly would have someone to talk to and to protect."

Molly stirred on her mat, stretched, and wagged her tail.

"Molly needs a companion just as much as I do to replace Lady Slipper."

"What are you going to name her?"

"Well, let's get together on that. But can't you just see our chocolate-brown cat riding on Molly's golden coat. And they're supposed to be very intelligent cats. Good hunters. They have been sailors' choice to rid ships of mice."

"How could she carry a cat? The cat would dig her claws into her back to hold on."

"Molly could be fitted with a little backpack. Lewis could make one and custom fit it. He knows every artisan in these woods."

"That's enough about our future," Josh said. "This day has been the longest day of our lives. Tomorrow we'll begin planning for Ted's memorial service alongside the river."

"The river," Joyce said. "The river grass that hypnotizes us as it sways under us as we wade. It has wrapped itself around us like a cocoon, and we flow with it. We have…dreamed the river, and the river responds. But the river knows it can calm. And, yes, calm our dreams. Even though this has been trauma, the river has cured me and I hope us."

Josh finally said, "I can actually feel the release, the letting go. Let's go up to the loft after this longest day of our lives."

Chapter 29

Molly awoke at the bird chatter around the feeder. She moved to the side window and saw that the squirrel baffle had slid down on the pole, and a squirrel had climbed onto the feeder and was feasting on the sunflower seeds. Ted never allowed this. Molly seldom climbed the stairs to the loft, but she felt that this demanded her attention. She nosed the door ajar and stood in the doorway until Joyce sat up and greeted her.

"You miss Ted, Molly. Come on, jump up here."

Molly hesitated and instead went to the window and strained to look out.

"Something out there?" Joyce came to her side and saw Molly's concern. "Josh will have to fix that." She sat on the end of the bed away from Josh, who was becoming restless. "Molly, Josh and I will live here now. We have crossed that dam that has separated us and will be husband and wife. This cabin is ours now. And yours. No one can replace Ted, but you can stand on the bank and enjoy fishing with Josh. Ted's bedroom, I don't know. Maybe that will be for our firstborn."

Molly put her paws onto the bed, and when Joyce bent down to pet her, she licked her fingers.

"We'll have a remembrance for Ted in a few days, and you'll be there as you were for Bill Catches' funeral."

Molly whined.

The funeral was only two days away on Saturday. The morning of the funeral coincided with the hatching of Hexagenia limbata, early this year. One hatch that both Josh and Ted never missed. Sunrise that day was 6:30 a.m.; moonset was 7:15 a.m. Johnson's hillside grave site would be prepared to welcome all who attended for early morning prayer and gathering. The funeral was scheduled to begin at 10:00. All the preliminaries had been planned by Josh's secretary at the pregnancy center. Ted's four daughters with their families were lodged in Gaylord, fifteen miles away. Most of Ted's acquaintances had passed on except a lady from Gary, Indiana, the former wife of one of the men who died in the aluminum extrusion plant where Ted worked in his youth. At ninety-two she enjoyed the same longevity as Ted. They had kept in touch with their yearly Christmas card. She'd fly up and go through the airport at Traverse City, then be chauffeured to the funeral site.

Chapter 30

When Oliver was returning from the Big Two-Hearted River for his return flight to Scotland, he stopped at the gas station in Vanderbilt and heard about Ted's passing. He'd attend the memorial service. What better stop than the Cold Spot Bar and at 7:00 p.m. He'd be on time for happy hour.

Sheriff Mad was leaning over the bar, searching for a napkin. "Hey, Connell, okay if I give my dog some of my hamburger?" His dog, Sergeant, was leashed onto one of the coat hooks on the front of the bar.

"Go ahead." As he spoke Lewis walked in.

"Hey, Sheriff. Bringing your dog to Ted's memorial service," Lewis said. He leaned over at the bar and petted Sergeant.

"Wouldn't go without him."

Connell, glancing out the window, said, "Look who just drove in, the marshal in his red SUV."

Oliver opened the bar door and stepped in.

"That's not the marshal," Connell said. "Oliver, welcome back. What brings you back here? How was it up there on the Fox and the Two-Hearted?"

Walking over to the bar, he said, "Seney was a fascinating town.

RAPTURE RIVER

I ended up back here as I was traveling south because I heard at the gas station of Ted's demise. I was reluctantly on my way to the airport to go home to Edinburgh. But that can wait. When is the remembrance ceremony?"

Connell filled his mug and set it on the bar. "Tapped from the top of the barrel. Almost equal to the drafts in Scotland. We try but the pubs back home are…well, take a swig."

Oliver gulped down half the mug. "Wonderful and, Sir Lewis, my pleasure to enjoy your company again."

"*Migwetch*, thank you. And the Fox and the Two-Hearted and Seney, Sir Oliver, was that good?"

"Seney was a fascinating town. I looked at *the burned-over stretch of hillside…and then walked down the railroad tracks to the bridge over the river. The river was there. It swirled against the log spiles of the bridge…looked down into the clear brown water, colored from the pebbly bottom, and watched the trout keeping themselves steady in the current with wavering fins.*[4] Those were Hemingway's words one hundred years ago, and the bridge and the river and the railroad tracks are still there. It was a joy. I didn't fish the Fox, but I waded the Two-Hearted. A kindly gentleman graciously granted me the use of his waders. And I waded some fast-running water. It was challenging. And this gracious man had a spare tent with him and said that if I came this far that I must sleep with the river, near her, on the bank, alongside the river, alongside her, and that as we slept, she would draw me in closer to her. And that I would dream of the river, and it would be the start of a romance never to be consummated, always desiring something that could never be touched. And next morning the courtship would begin as I waded into her waters. It was like talking to Hemingway. Now I see why he was attracted to waters. So, when is the funeral?"

"The funeral is two mornings away," Sheriff Mad said, "Saturday

---

[4] Hemingway, Ernest, "Big Two-Hearted River," *The Hemingway Stories* (New York: Scribner, 2021, Simon & Schuster publisher) p.79 Public Domain determined.

morning at ten, but I'd guess it will begin before sunrise in the gray light of predawn. The hill of Johnson's grave."

"I believe Ted mentioned that, and we had planned to wander up that way but never did conclude our intentions."

"I have an extra bedroom at my place. If you're looking for a place to stay."

"I welcome your hospitality, Sheriff Mad. Scotland can wait."

"Just follow me when we leave tonight."

Chapter 31

Josh woke on the morning of the funeral at 4:00. A restless night. When he opened the bedroom door, Molly was sitting there to greet him.

"Come in, Molly, and you can walk up with Joyce."

She went over to Joyce's bedside and licked her hand dangling over the side.

Joyce stirred and said, "Stay here with me, Molly. We'll go up later."

When Molly heard the cabin door slam, she jumped up on the foot of Josh's vacated side.

Josh stood on the porch, hesitating to travel the same path he shared with Ted over the years. His final walk on the path to the road, around the bend, and up to the hilltop, with Ted's spirit hovering above. He felt his presence.

He stepped down off the wooden porch onto solid ground. The sound of his boots on the wooden flooring broke the silence. Off in the distance an owl heralded another day beginning. When he reached the road, birds were still roosting, and above through the canopy of trees, starlight pierced the predawn darkness and lighted his way. He didn't need a flashlight. Darkness fit his somber mood.

ROBERT EDWARD SMITH

A faint morning hymn of the distant river riffled through the silence. Morning prayer in seminary was never as gripping as prayer offered up by nature.

And his thoughts began to wander over the many years with Ted and now with Joyce and Molly and drifted all the way back to his ordination into the priesthood and fly-fishing and how that brought him to this day of sorrow and yet of rejoicing and the love of Joyce uniting them into one and the miscarriage and Molly, who keeps interfering but also joining, uniting, loving both. And he began looking backward not forward to the celebration of Ted's passing and remembering that first meeting with Ted on the banks of the Black, knowing that those moments would be with him forever, and then meeting Joyce at Saint Peter the Fisherman, and immediately the animal attraction possessed them both as they stood outside the church by the statue of Saint Kateri Tekakwitha, and Ted not knowing but knowing that he would lose his confessor but gain and witness a growing relationship and then those two years nurtured by Molly and growing into caring and sharing each other and a mere dog, no, not a mere dog, a beautiful animal, elevating his own animal instincts and now at the passing of Ted that they would become one, but it took two deaths witnessed by Molly—a miscarriage and Ted's—all by the river and three other deaths along the river, and the river knew that those five deaths would enhance a love and resurrect the beginning of new life, and today would not be a mourning but a celebration of the new day arising with a ceremony to create new futures.

He stopped. Something was moving in the darkness. It stopped too. He moved on and whatever the darkness hid had been following up the trail to the hilltop. Must be a deer, maybe this year's fawn. An owl hooted. *A creature of wisdom telling him to stay awhile in this reverie of his growth, his metamorphosis like a butterfly emerging from its cocoon and alighting upon the closest most convenient perch, anything to hold onto that would promise its life but not knowing that the promise would have no guarantee, but he had grown away from his certainties, his absolute truths, because in life there are no absolutes except birth and death, and he had learned to enjoy the moment of now.*

He felt eyes out there, and suddenly they were gone, maybe behind a rock or one of the large maples on the hillside.

He sat on Johnson's gravestone at the top of the hill.

The sun was struggling this morning to arrest this darkness. At the first hint of predawn, the slightest hint of light, the hill gradually was born into grayness. There were no shadows yet allowing other worldly beings to cavort in their fairy ring. The oval clearing with only a boulder violating its space was teeming with ants, butterflies, and spiders. All jostling one another to get the best seat in this theatre, the drama that would play out. Birds—crows, mourning doves, red winged black birds—alighted on surrounding maples. A noisy chatter welcomed a rising sun and subsided as the sun peeked in. Outside the grassy barren hilltop and around the perimeter hidden behind the trees were the forest inhabitants gathering. Josh felt their presence. Would there be enough room for all the humans who would be gathering?

If the fairy ring surrounding the boulder were alive during the night, there was no trace, at least to Josh's eyes. But as the sky blued, the river was born again as light seeped into its depths—this day to welcome Ted.

Molly was the first guest to arrive at the crest of the hill. She approached Josh, moved past him to the outermost border of the fairy ring, and slowly circled around the burial site until Joyce reached the crest and sat with Josh on the boulder. They embraced in silence and looked down upon the Black River Valley.

Molly knew that she could not communicate with her master and mistress, but she understood the reason why they arrived at this hill above the river. This was not just any old hill above any old river. It carried with it the spirit of those who have lived and joined it. Sustained their lives from it, not only their lives but more as Josh had coupled his spirit with it. And she could see that the river meant many different things to different people. There had been life and death along the river. Lives that she touched and would always be connected to during her future life along her banks.

Joyce's thoughts meshed with Molly's and Josh's. All were migrating along the same course and evolving into the new life without the center of Ted, and Joyce could see but faintly the three progressing into this new excitement together without the calm assurance of Ted that possessed them, and she would eventually be an elder and look back upon her whole life, but now something strange was upon her sitting on that rock with Molly between her and Josh, and she felt that Molly was near human and she felt that before, but now it definitely made her sure about her, and she felt her not only physically but close to her thoughts if she could only talk, but then all of a sudden a breeze picked up while a passing cloud blocked the skylight, and a chilling thought rushed upon her—who would solve the mystery of the two men murdered on the river and when.

The hill had filled in quietly. The people surrounded the three who were the center of all—a half-circle with the view open to the river valley below and above the rising sun. Ted's four daughters gathered behind the rock. The sheriff, Lewis, Coop, Warden Mansfield, Marshal McClelan, Oliver, Reverend Jacob, and bartender Connell immediately behind. The villagers and Native Americans sat on Mother Earth. Above in the treetops and behind the maples was the Animal Kingdom honoring Molly, all filling in the half-circle.

All was quiet now as the sun bathed the valley in light and the river responded with shimmering, as if nervous and anticipating the ceremony above. The last person to arrive was the funeral attendant dressed in black and grasping the black box of Ted's remains. The congregation stood in respect to allow passage of the black box, which was handed to Josh, the funeral attendant then walking backward and merging into the congregation. Josh set the black box on the center of the boulder with Molly and Joyce beside him facing the hillside congregation.

"Does Ted need a eulogy?" he began. "Everyone here knew Ted. And if you didn't meet him, you heard about him.

"Off to my side here, sits Mahalia Jefferson. And I'll have to thank the two students of Joyce who carried her up here. She arrived yesterday in Traverse. Flew all the way up from Gary, Indiana, and arrived this morning by limousine. Mahalia and Josh kept in touch over the years with Christmas cards. He had known her and her husband, Clifton. When Ted was in his early twenties, he worked in an aluminum extrusion plant in Gary, Indiana. And he witnessed a tragedy in the cast house, where the molten metal was poured. A cask tipped and the metal spilled on the cement floor and took the lives of Clifton and two others. He witnessed these three men depart. The red-hot liquid stopped him from helping. He carried this the remainder of his life. And he told me to give in to the pull of the river and enjoy every minute of her presence. I did. This is how he would preach to us now. Nature's spirit heals—the Great Spirit."

He picked up the black box, opened the lid, and spread the dust over the rock. "The wind will scatter some, and the rain will wash the rest and fertilize Mother Earth. Amen."

Molly barked and the congregation answered, "Amen."

Chapter 32

The hill slowly owned itself again as the funeral procession departed and gave the hill back to itself. There would be a wake at the Cold Spot in Vanderbilt, courtesy of Mahalia. Libations and eats for the remainder of the day until the bar closed at midnight.

By 9:00 p.m. the crowd had dispersed, and only one table was occupied at the Cold Spot—Josh, Sheriff Mad, Marshal McClelan, Reverend Jacob, Oliver, and Joyce with Molly.

Oliver had asked the sheriff if he could extend his stay at his home, and the sheriff willingly encouraged him to stick around as long as he cared.

"Actually," the sheriff said, "I hoped you'd stay because I have a plan in mind."

Josh looked around the table at the assembly—a fallen priest, himself, a county sheriff, a minister of the serpent handlers, an agnostic Scottish professor, a federal marshal representing an oil company, and Joyce, a linguistics professor, with probably the most intelligent member of the crew, Molly.

"I'm fortunate that we're all assembled here," Sheriff Mad said. "There is and always will be the issue of the two murders along the river."

"Is there no solution?" Oliver asked. "The sheriff filled me in on all the details. But there is an answer to every dilemma. The quandary of deciding between life and death. The great Scottish philosopher Hume made the point that we react to our surroundings with our feelings first rather than our reasoning. So, whoever accomplished the murders is probably unable to cope with his intense feelings. Maybe about the river and its environs. These Holy Waters."

"I know who the murderer was," the sheriff said. "I've learned this from Coop and Lewis. Hardly reliable witnesses but…Lewis learned from Coop when he was talking to the butterflies." He paused, took a swig of his beer, and looked at Reverend Jacob. "And the reverend declared that he was bound by the confessional seal. Apparently, this spreads to the other religions from the Catholics. And I can guess the murderer from that alone."

"We need a courtroom and a trial," Reverend Jacob said. "Let us meet at the Signs Followers chapel at 6:00 p.m. on Monday to resolve this matter. This may be a sudden intrusion, but in the silence of the chapel, along with prayer, we may be enlightened. And grace may be bestowed upon us. Grace shows up where you least expect it."

All agreed but Joyce. "I'll be absent, but Molly can take my place."

Chapter 33

The sun was dropping over the pines in the west, imprisoning the Signs Followers church in long bar-like shadows. The sheriff drove in with Oliver followed by Marshal McClelan, and Josh with Molly. The reverend was standing in front of the church door. Quietly all assembled around him.

"May you please kneel," Reverend Jacob said.

All knelt around the reverend elevated on the top step.

Molly sat on her haunches in the middle between Oliver and the sheriff with Marshal McClelan and Josh at both ends.

"You only have to walk up these three wooden steps to enter the sanctuary. We have a semicircle here. In the middle is an animal who may know more than any of us humans. Let her spirit fill us with her insight so that we may be the judge, court, and jury of the murderer of these two innocent victims. May the Holy Spirit fill the soul of the guilty with remorse and atonement. Amen."

"Amen."

Molly responded by raising her paw and tapping on the bottom step.

They entered the chapel with Molly leading and following the reverend to the altar. Reverend Jacob lit the kerosene lamp on the altar. "We have no pews. I spread these chairs so we can all sit here and commence with the trial. Molly can sit next to Josh and Sheriff

Mad, and Oliver and Marshal McClelan on the other side. So how should we begin? And who should be the moderator of our trial?"

Molly looked at Oliver.

"How brilliant her insight," the reverend said. "Have an outsider without our prejudices begin."

"And I shall accept your confirmation," Oliver said. "Thank you, Reverend. And Molly for your unsaid recommendation."

Marshal McClelan interrupted. "I have my reservations."

"But," Josh said, "would a long, drawn-out trial be good for the oil company?"

"No. The environmental crackpots would flood these virgin lands on one of their holy pilgrimages."

"So, let's proceed and see what we come up with."

"Okay," the marshal said, "I'll go along with it. No promises."

"I graciously accept your affirmation, Marshal. And I understand the weight of your office and how heavily it falls upon you. I feel you take your position not lightly, and compromises could tarnish your reputation."

Marshal McClelan nodded.

"Thank you, Marshal," Oliver said. "Sheriff Mad briefed me on the perpetrator of these grisly murders. The guilty party, according to the sheriff, was placed in an orphanage, a Catholic orphanage, at a very young age. Unfortunately, that institution had a history of molestations." He stopped. Glanced at Josh. "The said guilty party was institutionalized, for lack of a better word, from the ages of thirteen to seventeen. The sheriff knew the family."

"And he looked upon these waters as being holy waters," Sheriff Mad said.

"He did," Reverend Jacob said. "He loved this river. It was the only family attachment that he owned. Poor soul. And his early abuse only heightened his anger. I can say this about him: he is a good human being. But society demands a sentence for murder."

"So, what is the solution?" the marshal asked.

"Banishment," Oliver said.

"Banishment! What the hell," the marshal shouted.

"Allow me to elucidate. Banishment would be his hell, Marshal. Banishment was a common tool employed to rid Scotland of its criminals. They were banished to Australia and America."

At the click of the church door, Oliver looked at the entrance. Lewis stood in the doorway dressed in his finest leather deer hide. He walked silently down the aisle in his moccasins, while the assembled court members all rose.

"Ah, Sir Lewis," Oliver said. "We welcome your presence."

"Thank you, Oliver. I have heard you all talking. This chapel has big ears," Lewis said. "And I feel that this is a fair sentence for the murderer." He glanced at Marshal McClelan. "Some of the wells are being closed and the land restored as your company promised our council, and we know about broken promises. So, the oil company could remain and become more friendly to the lands."

"If this isn't a kangaroo court. I don't know what is," Sheriff Mad said. "The legal system and justice no longer exist. We must preserve our own lands. We have the responsibility to sentence the murderer but prove that he will not repeat. We are the judge and jury. But we'd have to prove that he's dead, not hiding out. I could ask the coroner and the funeral director for a slight favor. They owe me. We could claim a bear has attacked the murderer and we recovered the remains. Proven, of course, by a fabricated DNA test. The boys in the Bear Clan might help us there. The damn federal government lies like hell, so why can't we. But we tell honest lies. This kangaroo court is adjourned." And Molly barked.

Part 3
Next Year

Next year

Ontario, Canada

"All aboard, last call," the conductor shouted as the train chugged out of the station at Sault Ste. Marie, Ontario, and headed north into the Canadian wilderness. When Dean bought his ticket on that May morning, he had decided to be dropped off at Mile 213, where the train crossed a bridge over the Attawapiskat River. He'd trade one river for another. But no river could replace the Black, the river he had grown up in and that grew into him. A river he had to abandon to remain free—an orphan without a river.

The train came to a halt on marker 213. The porter stood in the open baggage car and pitched his backpack onto the gravel bed along the tracks. Dean climbed down the steel ladder and, when he reached the bottom rung, jumped onto the gravel.

"Sure you're making the right choice?" the porter asked. "This is bear country. Can be mean critters. Last year were two bear attacks. Both died of…well, real bad and suffered. How long you plan on staying?"

Dean shrugged. "Don't know."

"We make the line once a week. Come up Monday. Back Friday. Between one and three p.m. So, all you do is stand in the middle of the tracks on this here straightaway, wave and holler, and we'll get ya. Good luck. Y'all only got a couple of hours left of daylight. So, get yourself going."

"Thanks." Dean lugged his backpack off the gravel onto the grassy bank along the tracks, sat down, and counted the cars, all twenty-three, as the train crossed the trestle over the Attawapiskat River and disappeared around the bend. The surrounding maple trees were beginning to bud, a few weeks behind the leafing trees back home. The river was barely visible down the steep, forested hillside. Scattered patches of snow would all melt after a few more days like today. From the canyon below, the river roared. He had a new river, a more turbulent river, deep-banked and foaming, but not the Black. He took out his jackknife, unfolded the blade, picked up a broken maple limb, just the right size for his walking stick, and began whittling.

He shaved the bark off the branch and ran his fingers along the shaft, not as smooth as the bone handle of his jackknife. Now he had a rod, something solid to hold onto, but nothing could fill that hollow pit in his chest. And he felt alone. If he were lost or injured here, who'd rescue him? He stopped whittling, held the knife loosely in his palm, and stared at the inscription carved into the bone handle—To my son Dean on his 12th birthday. The image of his father appeared in the shiny face of the blade. And he heard his father's voice again calling out, "Dean, Dean," when he was a little boy, lost along the river. His father found him before, but now no one even knew his whereabouts. And he yelled out over all the bleakness, "I done wrong, Daddy, and I'm sorry. You know I'm sorry. I always remember Mama, and I see her dying of cancer. So terrible. And then, Daddy, you followed her. You missed her more. I had to fight on all by myself, and in that

RAPTURE RIVER

orphanage it was real bad. And all I had was the river to escape to for comfort and forget." He closed his knife and put it into his pocket and took out his map and compass. *"I'll be seeing you soon, Daddy."* He had to make camp before the sun set. Maybe he'd meet up with a squaw in these woods and live off the wilderness and start over.

He picked up his backpack, glanced along the lonely railroad tracks, and began hiking down the canyon wall to the river, bracing himself with his new staff.

Next Year

Morning. Upper Black River on the High Banks of the Blue Lakes.

From the side of a hill laced with red pine, the bear watched her three cubs foraging for mice and grubs under spring flowers of trailing arbutus. She lifted her nose, picked up human scent, and peered through trees at two humans sidling down the steep slope. One of the humans was carrying a bundled blanket. The bear turned toward the river. Sun's rays pieced through voids in the overhead canopy and splashed sparkle onto water. High above, mayflies were spinning early on this mild spring morning. The humans stopped on the riverbank near the water, laid the blanket on grass, and unwrapped a black-headed cub like her own. They knelt down close together. The bear heard voices.

"That smile, yours," Josh said, "and her hair."

"She is both of us," Joyce said, "and I hope as she grows that she'll have your intensity and your courage."

"Courage?"

"Yes, your courage. Courage to follow the ways of her heart."

"And your gentleness and compassion. And your loving, affectionate nature. You gave us so much. Now her baptism."

"First her *Mnwaabmewzid,* her blessing," Joyce said.

Joyce opened her deerskin pouch and picked out an abalone shell. She cleared a spot on the ground between them, brushing the twigs and grass aside, creating a dip where she set the shell. She removed grayish-green leaves of sage from the pouch, sprinkled them into the bowl, and struck a match to light them. The smoke wafted up in thin spirals. With the tail feather of a red-tailed hawk, she fanned the fumes over the infant. Then gripping the spine of the feather in one hand, she swiped her fingers of her other hand along its length to the tip, rhythmically repeating several times as she chanted in Ojibwa.

A breeze picked up and a veil of smoke hovered above, drifted down upon the infant, and alighted upon her. They sat motionless. Joyce finally looked up at Josh and said, "Her spirit is here, now. The wind is whispering her name… Her name is Sing the Wind… We'll call her Windy."

"Mariah," Josh said. "They call the wind Mariah."

"Mariah. Let it be. Nickname, Windy." Joyce dipped her finger into the ashes and smeared Mariah's forehead.

They stood. Both were dressed in blue jeans and red flannel shirts. "Now for her baptism," Josh said. "Let's keep our hiking boots on. It's gravelly out there. Be one and carefree with water, feel it, possess its wetness." Josh carried the infant in the crook of his arm, and they walked out into the river. The icy clearness swishing around and tugging at them as Joyce grasped his shirt. They stopped when the water was up to Josh's waist in midstream. He steadied himself, cradled the infant in one arm, and lowered her head to the river, the baby squirming and smiling. He cupped his palm, dipped it into the river, and sprinkled a few drops on her forehead.

"I baptize…"

Now only the river can continue telling her story. But she can only tell the lives of those who touch her waters. And she will not tell all she knows because she understands that some of her stories we couldn't bear. But to the stories she does tell us, we respond like little children and say, "Tell us more."

Epilogue

Ten Years Later

In ten years, the river was feeling a new story. The story of two children, Windy and her little brother, Zachery. Windy and Zach both missed Molly, but their mom told them that it was time for Molly to join the spirit world. They still had the cat, Whisper, who also missed Molly. She had ridden on Molly's back, clawing onto the vest Lewis made.

"We like Lewis, Mom," Windy said as she was helping her load the woodburning stove. "He walks real slow with his big stick, and he tells us stories about Molly and Coop and the butterflies. Who was Coop, Mom?"

"He was an old man who lived in the swamp. He's in the spirit world with Molly."

"Mom, I have to tell you a secret. Mom, when Zack and me go up to the top of the hill just before dark, we hide behind the trees, and I always whisper, and I put my finger on Zack's lips and go *Shhh,* and he knows to be quiet, and we watch the moon come up. And Whisper follows us. We tell her to go home, but she won't, so she hides with us. And sometimes we see Molly and a lot of other animals. And even a real big man sits on the big rock. Mom, why do you have tears? Do you feel sad?"

"*Gaa wii*, no. Oh, I don't know," she said, wiping her wet cheeks with the back of her hand. "I'm thinking of Molly, and I miss her too."

"Mom," Windy said, grasping her hand and looking up at her, "you don't have to worry about us. Lewis is there too. He just comes. And he sits hiding with us, with Whisper in his lap, and he smiles and Whisper purrs. And we never talk. After we come down, Lewis tells us that we looked at the spirit world.

"And sometimes we want you and Dad to go with us. And we asked Lewis if we should ask you and Dad, and he said maybe."

And the story flows on, the river anxious for the next chapter.

Acknowledgments

First of all, I'd like to thank the Black River with my following attempt at a free verse poem:

I have fly-fished the Black River near Onaway, Michigan,
for more than seventy years.
Sought shelter from the Black's rain
beneath the cedar trees on its banks.
Slept under the white pines on its
hillsides on hot summer afternoons.
Drank its cooling waters.
Cast flies on its silvery surface by the light of a full moon.
Waded through its dense fog.
Caught the last mid-May snowfall with
flakes as large as hummingbirds.
And stumbled into its icy waters.
Consequently, I have dreamed the river.
And my dreams have transcended the
Black into my mythological river.
—Robert Edward Smith

Even though the river initiated my dreaming the novel, I catch myself most frequently recalling the characters in the novel, including Molly along with her Animal Kingdom. I've been with them, off and on, for a few years, and I regret having to depart from their company. I love each and every one of them. The dilemma of magical realism is that the further in you go, the better it gets; but also, the deeper it gets, and the harder to get out.

Some of my geographical directions along the river were vague, no, downright inaccurate, but I apologize, and I know the river, the main character, will forgive me. Maybe it's my unconscious reaction to exposing my favorite fishing stretches of the Black. Fishermen are known to be liars. So it goes.

However, I didn't arrive at my novel's destination overnight. In May 2018, I completed the webinar "Constructing a Novel" sponsored by Penguin Random House in London, England. I owe many thanks to Barbara Henderson and Molly Crawford there for the initial editing of the novel. Thanks also to my writing workshop instructors at the University of Iowa Summer Writing Festival over the past thirty years; and also to Tom Jenks, who encouraged me to write at his workshop, Advanced Short Fiction, in Chicago in 2004. And thanks to the Bear River Writers' Conferences in northern Michigan on the shores of Walloon Lake, Hemingway country. Three of my short stories were published in the *Bear River Review*, the 2009, 2010, and 2011 issues. And I fondly remember the 2015 Bread Loaf Environmental Writers' Conference, in particular, the cordial atmosphere in the Barn, where I improved my public speaking skills.

So, all this brings me to my final comment. After researching the self-publishing houses, I decided on Outskirts Press. My author representative was Dana Nelson, the rock I leaned on throughout the publishing process. Thanks to her and the staff at Outskirts Press.

And thanks to my readers. I hope you enjoyed the ride.

Credits

Thanks to all the publishers who patiently guided me through the maze of the permissions network; namely, The University of South Carolina Press, Wesleyan University Press, Simon & Schuster, W. W. Norton, and Penguin Random House. Thanks also to Pixabay for the images.

Quotes and Permissions

Note 1. The leap between the sacred and profane is as thin as fishing line; and is part of the mystery on this river of life… Joy Harjo, an enrolled member of the Muscogee Tribe, from *The Woman Who Fell from the Sky: Poems*.

Permission granted from W. W. Norton by Robert Shatzkin to use as my epigraph dated February 16, 2024.

[1] Harjo, Joy. *The Woman Who Fell from the Sky: Poems* (Copyright 1994 by Joy Harjo, First published as a Norton paperback,1996) p. 75 e-book, "Fishing." Used by Permission.

Note 2. *Anyone who lives for long in any untouched landscape—especially in wide, stark, dramatic, primitive country—will find that, whether he recognizes it or not, the land becomes part of his religion. Probably forms its foundations. Ancient or modern man, it makes no difference. City dwellers, cut off from the land, naturally tend to disagree. Two and a half centuries ago, city dweller Alexander Pope wrote,*

> *Lo, the poor Indian! Whose untutored mind*
> *Sees God in clouds, or hears him in the wind*

—though Pope did allow the poor Indian, through "simple nature… an humbler heaven." A modern tutored Indian might respond,

> *Lo, poor Alex Pope! Whose overtutored mind*
> *Cannot see God in clouds, or hear him in the wind.*

Anyway, for those in touch with the land, its substance reaches deep into their souls.

[2] Fletcher, Colin. *River: One Man's Journey Down the Colorado, Source to Sea* (First Vintage Departures Edition, A Division of Penguin Random House, May 1998), pp. 215-216. Fair Use determined. Permission granted from Penguin Random House, to be quoted in the body of the text only, by Beau Sullivan dated January 29, 2024.

Chapter 21. "Recently a four-page, handwritten letter of Hemingway's was auctioned off for $237,055. He signed it Ernie."

"Say again," Connell yelled over the bar. He walked over to Oliver. "Let me see." He read the note. "Auctioned by Nate D. Sanders, $237,055. Why would anyone?" (Auction closed on Thursday,

August 31, 2023, by Nate D. Sanders Auctions, Fine Autographs & Memorabilia)

> Note 3. *I give you this one thought to keep—*
> *I am with you still, and do not weep,*
> *I am a thousand winds that blow,*
> *I am the diamond glints on snow,*
> *I am the sunlight on ripened grain,*
> *I am the gentle autumn rain.*
> *When you awaken in the morning hush,*
> *I am the swift, uplifting rush*
> *Of quiet birds in circled flight.*
> *I am the soft stars that shine at night,*
> *Do not think of me as gone—*
> *I am with you still—in each cold new dawn.*

[3] "Native American Prayer for the Grieving," author unknown, churchgists.com. A revised version of the original poem "Do Not Stand by My Grave and Weep" by Mary Elizabeth Frye, which was written in 1932 and never published. The author intended it for public use.

Note 4. *'the burned-over stretch of hillside…and then walked down the railroad tracks to the bridge over the river. The river was there. It swirled against the log spiles of the bridge…looked down into the clear brown water, colored from the pebbly bottom, and watched the trout keeping themselves steady in the current with wavering fins.*

[4] Hemingway, Ernest. "Big Two-Hearted River," from *The Hemingway Stories* (New York: Scribner, 2021, Simon & Schuster publisher) p. 79. In Public Domain as determined by Simon & Schuster.

Bibliography

Scattered throughout the novel are Native American expressions. The following dictionary was my main source.

Rhodes, Richard A. Eastern Ojibwa-Chippewa-Ottawa Dictionary. Berlin, New York: Mouton de Gruyter publisher, 1993.